In an instant he was the center of a hurricane of stabbing spears and lashing clubs. But he moved in a blinding blur of steel. Spears bent on his armor or swished empty air, and his sword sang its death song. The fighting madness of his race was upon him, and with a red mist of unreasoning fury wavering before his blazing eyes, he cleft skulls, smashed breasts, severed limbs, ripped out entrails, and littered the deck like a shambles with a ghastly harvest of brains and blood.

Invulnerable in his armor, his back against the mast, he heaped mangled corpses at his feet until his enemies gave back panting in rage and fear. Then as they lifted their spears to cast them, and he tensed himself to leap and die in the midst of them, a shrill cry froze the lifted arms. They stood like statues, the black giants poised for the spear casts, the mailed swordsman with his dripping blade.

Chronological order of the CONAN series:

CONAN
CONAN OF CIMMERIA
CONAN THE FREEBOOTER
CONAN THE WANDERER
CONAN THE ADVENTURER
CONAN THE BUCCANEER
CONAN THE WARRIOR
CONAN THE USURPER
CONAN THE CONQUEROR
CONAN THE AVENGER
CONAN OF AQUILONIA
CONAN OF THE ISLES
CONAN THE SWORDSMAN
CONAN THE LIBERATOR
CONAN THE SWORD OF SKELOS
CONAN THE ROAD OF KINGS
CONAN THE REBEL
CONAN AND THE SPIDER GOD

Illustrated CONAN novels:

CONAN AND THE SORCERER
CONAN: THE FLAME KNIFE
CONAN THE MERCENARY
THE TREASURE OF TRANICOS

Other CONAN novels:

THE BLADE OF CONAN
THE SPELL OF CONAN

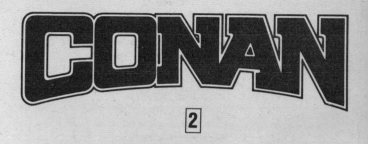

CONAN

2

OF CIMMERIA

BY ROBERT E. HOWARD,
L. SPRAGUE DE CAMP AND LIN CARTER

ACE BOOKS, NEW YORK

The Curse of the Monolith was first published under the title *Conan and the Cenotaph* in *Worlds of Fantasy*, Vol. 1, No. 1, 1968; copyright © 1968 by Galaxy Publishing Corp.

The Bloodstained God was rewritten by L. Sprague de Camp from an original story by Robert E. Howard called *The Trail of the Blood-Stained God*, laid in modern Afghanistan. It was first published in *Tales of Conan*, by Robert E. Howard and L. Sprague de Camp, Gnome Press, Inc., copyright © 1955 by Gnome Press, Inc.

The Frost Giant's Daughter was first published in slightly different form under the title *Gods of the North* in *The Fantasy Fan* for March, 1934; it was reprinted in this form in *Fantastic Universe Science Fiction* for December, 1956. Revised by Robert E. Howard and later by L. Sprague de Camp, it was reprinted under its present title in *Fantasy Fiction* for August, 1953; copyright © 1953 by Future Publications, Inc.; and in *The Coming of Conan*, by Robert E. Howard, Gnome Press, Inc., 1953.

The Lair of the Ice Worm is published here for the first time.

Queen of the Black Coast was first published in *Weird Tales* for May, 1934; copyright © 1934 by Popular Fiction Publishing Co.; it was reprinted in *Avon Fantasy Reader No. 8*, 1948 and in *The Coming of Conan*.

The Vale of Lost Women was first published in *Magazine of Horror No. 15* for Spring, 1967; copyright © 1967 by Health Knowledge, Inc.

The Castle of Terror is published here for the first time.

The Snout in the Dark, rewritten by L. Sprague de Camp and Lin Carter from an outline and the first half of the rough draft of a story by Robert E. Howard, is published here for the first time.

The biographical paragraphs between the stories are based upon A Probable Outline of Conan's Career by P. Schuyler Miller and Dr. John D. Clark, published in *The Hyborian Age*, 1938, and on the expanded version of this essay, An Informal Biography of Conan the Cimmerian, by P. Schuyler Miller, Dr. John D. Clark and L. Sprague de Camp, published in *Amra*, Vol. 2, No. 4; copyright © 1959 by G. H. Scithers; used by permission of G. H. Scithers.

CONAN OF CIMMERIA

An Ace Book / published by arrangement with
the Estate of Robert E. Howard

PRINTING HISTORY
Ace edition / October 1982

ISBN: 0-441-11453-9

Ace Books are published by The Berkley Publishing Group,
200 Madison Avenue, New York, New York 10016.
The name "ACE" and the "A" logo
are trademarks belonging to Charter Communications, Inc.

PRINTED IN THE UNITED STATES OF AMERICA

Contents

Pages 6 and 7: A map of the world of Conan in the Hyborian Age, based upon notes and sketches by Robert E. Howard and upon previous maps by P. Schuyler Miller, John D. Clark, David Kyle, and L. Sprague de Camp, with a map of Europe and adjacent regions superimposed for reference.

Introduction

ROBERT ERVIN HOWARD (1906–36) was born in Peaster, Texas, and lived most of his life in Cross Plains, in the center of Texas between Abilene and Brownwood. During his last decade, this prolific and versatile writer turned out a large volume of what was then called ''pulp fiction'' —sport, detective, western, historical, adventure, weird, and ghost stories, as well as his many stories of adventure fantasy. Edgar Rice Burroughs, Robert W. Chambers, Harold Lamb, Talbot Mundy, Jack London, and H. P. Lovecraft (of whom he was a pen pal) all influenced him. At the age of thirty, he ended a promising literary career by suicide.

Howard's adventure fantasies belong to a kind of fiction called heroic fantasy, or sometimes swordplay-and-sorcery stories. Such stories are laid in a world not as it is or was but as it ought to have been. The setting may be the world as it is conceived to have been long ago, or as it will be in the distant future, or on another planet, or in another dimension. In such a world, magic works and spirits are real, but modern science and technology are essentially unknown. Either they have not yet been discovered, or they have been forgotten. Men are mighty, women are beautiful, problems are simple, and life is adventurous.

When well done, such tales furnish the purest *fun* to be found in modern fiction. They are designed primarily to entertain, not to educate, uplift, or convert to some faith or ideology. They derive ultimately from the myths, legends, and epics of ancient times and primitive peoples. After several centuries of neglect, William Morris revived the genre in England in the 1880s. Early in this century, Lord Dunsany and Eric R. Eddison made further contributions to the field. A notable recent addition to it has been the *Lord of the Rings* trilogy by J. R. R. Tolkien.

The appearance of the American magazines *Weird Tales* in 1923 and *Unknown Worlds* in 1939 created new markets for heroic fantasy, and many notable stories in the genre were published. Among these, Howard's tales were outstanding. Howard wrote several series of heroic fantasies, most of them published in *Weird Tales*. Of these, the longest and most popular series comprised the Conan stories. Eighteen Conan stories were published in Howard's lifetime. Eight others, from complete manuscripts to mere fragments and outlines, have been discovered among Howard's papers since 1950.

Late in 1951, I stumbled upon a cache of Howard's manuscripts in the apartment of the then literary agent for Howard's estate. These included a few unpublished Conan stories, which I edited for publication. Other manuscripts have been found in more recent years by Glenn Lord, literary agent for the Howard estate, in collections of Howard's papers.

The incomplete state of the Conan saga has tempted me and others to add to it, as Howard might have done had he lived. In the early 1950s, I rewrote the manuscripts of four of Howard's unpublished adventure stories, with medieval or modern settings, to turn them into Conan stories. More recently, my colleagues Björn Nyberg and Lin Carter have collaborated with me in the completion of the stories that Howard left unfinished and in the composition of pastiches, based upon hints in Howard's notes and letters, to fill the gaps in the saga. The reader must judge how successful our posthumous collaboration with Howard had been.

Before he undertook the writing of the Conan stories, Howard constructed a pseudo-history of Conan's world.

with the geography, ethnography, and political units clearly worked out. It is partly the concreteness of Howard's imaginary world that gives his stories their vividness and fascination—his sharp, gorgeous, consistent vision of "a purple and golden and crimson universe where anything can happen—except the tedious." He incorporated this plan in a long essay, "The Hyborian Age," which is printed in two parts in the volumes *Conan* and *Conan the Avenger* of this series.

According to Howard's scheme, Conan lived, loved, and plunged into his desperate adventures about twelve thousand years ago, eight thousand years after the sinking of Atlantis and seven thousand before the beginnings of recorded history.

In this time (according to Howard) the western parts of the main continent of the Eastern Hemisphere were occupied by the Hyborian kingdoms. These comprised a galaxy of states set up by northern invaders, the Hyborians, three thousand years earlier on the ruins of the evil empire of Acheron. South of the Hyborian kingdoms lay the quarreling city-states of Shem. Beyond Shem slumbered the ancient, sinister kingdom of Stygia, the rival and partner of Acheron in the days of the latter's bloodstained glory. Further south, yet, beyond deserts and veldts, were barbarous black kingdoms. North of the Hyborians lay the barbarian lands of Cimmeria, Hyperborea, Vanaheim, and Asgard. West, along the ocean, were the fierce, savage Picts. To the east glittered the Hyrkanian kingdoms, of which the mightiest was Turan.

About 500 years after the time of Conan the Great, most of these realms were swept away by barbarian invasions and migrations. After some centuries during which the earth supported a drastically shrunken population of wandering, quarreling barbarians, civilization—what was left of it—was further overwhelmed by the last advance of the glaciers from the poles and by a convulsion of nature like that which had previously destroyed Atlantis. At this time, the North and Mediterranean Seas were formed, the great inland Vilayet Sea shrank to the dimensions of the present

Caspian, and vast areas of West Africa arose from beneath the waves of the Atlantic. Mankind sank to the most primitive savagery. After the retreat of the ice of this glaciation, civilization again revived and recorded history began.

Conan was a gigantic barbarian adventurer who roistered, brawled, and battled his way across half the prehistoric world, to rise at last to the throne of a mighty realm. The son of a blacksmith in the bleak, backward northern country of Cimmeria, Conan was born on a battlefield in that land of rugged hills and somber skies. As a youth, he took part in the sack of the Aquilonian frontier settlement of Venarium.

Later, joining a band of Æsir in a raid into Hyperborea, Conan was captured by the Hyperboreans. Escaping from the Hyperborean slave pen, he wandered south into the kingdom of Zamora. For several years he made a precarious living there and in the adjacent lands of Corinthia and Nemedia as a thief. (See map, pages 6 and 7.) Green to civilization and quite lawless by nature, he made up for his lack of subtlety and sophistication by natural shrewdness and by the herculean physique he had inherited from his father.

Tiring of this starveling existence, Conan enlisted as a mercenary soldier in the armies of Turan. For the next two years he traveled widely, as far east as the fabled lands of Meru and Khitai. He also refined his archery and horsemanship, both of which had been at best indifferent up to the time of his joining the Turanians. It is during the later part of his Turanian service that the present volume begins.

L. Sprague de Camp

CONAN
OF CIMMERIA

The Curse of the Monolith

Following the events of "The City of Skulls" (in the volume Conan), *Conan rises to the rank of captain in the Turanian service. His growing repute as an irresistible fighter and a good man in a tight spot, however, instead of leading to soft jobs with large pay for little work, causes King Yildiz's generals to choose him for particularly hazardous missions. One of these takes him thousands of miles to eastward, to fabled Khitai.*

1.

THE SHEER CLIFFS of dark stone closed about Conan the Cimmerian like the sides of a trap. He did not like the way their jagged peaks loomed against the few faint stars, which glittered like the eyes of spiders down upon the small camp on the flat floor of the valley. Neither did he like the chill, uneasy wind that whistled across the stony heights and prowled about the campfire. It caused the flames to lean and flicker, sending monstrous black shadows writhing across the rough stone walls of the nearer valley side.

On the other side of the camp, colossal redwoods, which had been old when Atlantis sank beneath the waves eight thousand years before, rose amid thickets of bamboo and clumps of rhododendron. A small stream meandered out of the woods, murmured past the camp, and wandered off into the forest again. Overhead, a layer of haze or high fog drifted across the tops of the cliffs, drowning the light of the fainter stars and making the brighter ones seem to weep.

Something about this place, thought Conan, stank of fear and of death. He could almost smell the acrid odor of terror on the breeze. The horses felt it, too. They nickered plaintively, pawed the earth, and rolled white eyeballs at the dark beyond the circle of the fire. The beasts were close to nature. So was Conan, the young barbarian warrior from the bleak hills of Cimmeria. Like his, their senses were more delicately turned to the aura of evil than were the senses of city-bred men like the Turanian troopers he had led into this deserted vale.

The soldiers sat about the fire, sharing the last of this night's ration of wine from goatskin bags. Some laughed and boasted of the amorous feats they would do in the silken bagnios of Aghrapur upon their return. Others, weary from a long day's hard ride, sat silently, staring at the fire and yawning. Soon they would settle down for the night, rolled in their heavy cloaks. With their heads pillowed on saddlebags, they would lie in a loose circle about the hissing fire, while two of their number stood guard with their powerful Hyrkanian bows strung and ready. They sensed nothing of the sinister force that hovered about the valley.

Standing with his back to the nearest of the giant redwoods, Conan wrapped his cloak more closely about him against the dank breeze from the heights. Although his troopers were well-built men of good size, he towered half a head over the tallest of them, while his enormous breadth of shoulder made them seem puny by comparison. His square-cut black mane escaped from below the edges of his spired, turban-wound helmet, and the deep-set blue eyes in his dark, scarred face caught glints of red from the firelight.

Sunk in one of his fits of melancholy gloom, Conan

16

silently cursed King Yildiz, the well-meaning but weak Turanian monarch who had sent him on this ill-omened mission. Over a year had passed since he had taken the oath of allegiance to the king of Turan. Six months before, he had been lucky enough to earn this king's favor; with the help of a fellow-mercenary, Juma the Kushite, he had rescued Yildiz's daughter Zosara from the mad god-king of Meru. He had brought the princess, more or less intact, to her affianced bridegroom, Khan Kujala of the nomadic Kuigar horde.

When Conan returned to Yildiz's glittering capital of Aghrapur, he had found the monarch generous enough in his gratitude. Both he and Juma had been raised to captain. But, whereas Juma had obtained a coveted post in the Royal Guard, Conan had been rewarded with yet another arduous, perilous mission. Now, as he recalled these events, he sourly contemplated the fruits of success.

Yildiz had entrusted the Cimmerian giant with a letter to King Shu of Kusan, a minor kingdom in western Khitai. At the head of forty veterans, Conan had accomplished the immense journey. He had traversed hundreds of leagues of bleak Hyrkanian steppe and skirted the foothills of the towering Talakma Mountains. He had threaded his way through the windy deserts and swampy jungles bordering the mysterious realm of Khitai, the easternmost land of which the men of the West had heard.

Arrived in Kusan at last, Conan had found the venerable and philosophical King Shu a splendid host. While Conan and his warriors were plied with exotic food and drink and furnished with willing concubines, the king and his advisers decided to accept King Yildiz's offer of a treaty of friendship and trade. So the wise old king had handed Conan a gorgeous scroll of gilded silk. Thereon were inscribed, in the writhing ideographs of Khitai and the gracefully slanted characters of Hyrkania, the formal replies and felicitations of the Khitan king.

17

Besides a silken purse full of Khitan gold, King Shu had also furnished Conan with a high noble of his court, to guide them as far as the western borders of Khitai. But Conan had not liked this guide, this Duke Feng.

The Khitan was a slim, dainty, foppish little man with a soft, lisping voice. He wore fantastical silken garments, unsuited to rugged riding and camping, and drenched his exquisite person in heavy perfume. He never soiled his soft, long-nailed hands with any of the camp chores, but instead kept his two servants busy day and night ministering to his comfort and dignity.

Conan looked down upon the Khitan's habits with a hard-bitten barbarian's manly contempt. The duke's slanting black eyes and purring voice reminded him of a cat, and he often told himself to watch this little princeling for treachery. On the other hand, he secretly envied the Khitan his exquisitely cultivated manners and easy charm. This fact led Conan to resent the duke even more; for, although his Turanian service had given Conan some slight polish, he was still at heart the blunt, boorish young barbarian. He would have to be careful of this sly little Duke Feng.

2.

"Do I disturb the profound meditations of the nobly born commander?" purred a soft voice.

Conan started and snatched at the hilt of his tulwar before he recognized the person of Duke Feng, wrapped to the lip in a voluminous cloak of pea-green velvet. Conan started to growl a contemptuous curse. Then, remembering his ambassadorial duties, he turned the oath into a formal welcome that sounded unconvincing even in his own ears.

"Perhaps the princely captain is unable to sleep?" murmured Feng, appearing not to notice Conan's ungracious-

18

ness. Feng spoke fluent Hyrkanian. This was one reason for his having been dispatched to guide Conan's troop, for Conan's command of the singsong Khitan tongue was little more than a smattering. Feng continued:

"This person is so fortunate as to possess a sovereign remedy for sleeplessness. A gifted apothecary concocted it for me from an ancient recipe: a decoction of lily buds ground into cinnamon and spiced with poppy seeds . . ."

"No, nothing," growled Conan. "I thank you, Duke, but it's something about this accursed place. Some uncanny premonition keeps me wakeful when, after a long day's ride, I should be as weary as a stripling after his first night's bout of love."

The duke's features moved a trifle, as if he winced at Conan's crudity—or was it merely a flicker of the firelight? In any case, he suavely replied, "I think I understand the misgivings of the excellent commander. Nor are such disquieting emotions unusual in this—ah—this legend-fraught valley. Many men have perished here."

"A battlefield, eh?" grunted Conan.

The duke's narrow shoulders twitched beneath the green cloak. "Nay, nothing like that, my heroic Western friend. This spot lies near the tomb of an ancient king of my people: King Hsia of Kusan. He caused his entire royal guard to be beheaded and their heads buried with him, that their spirits should continue to serve him in the next world. The common superstition, however, avers that the ghosts of these guardsmen march in review, up and down this valley." The soft voice dropped even lower. "Legend also states that a magnificent treasure of gold and precious jewels was buried with him; and this tale I believe to be true."

Conan pricked up his ears. "Gold and gems, eh? Has it ever been found, this treasure?"

The Khitan surveyed Conan for a moment with an oblique, contemplative gaze. Then, as if having reached some private decision, he replied, "No, Lord Conan; for the precise location of the trove is not known—save to one man."

Conan's interest was quite visible now. "To whom?" he demanded bluntly.

The Khitan smiled. "To my unworthy self, of course."

"Crom and Erlik! If you've known where this loot was hidden, why haven't you dug it up ere now?"

"My people are haunted by superstitious fears of a curse laid upon the site of the old king's tomb, which is marked by a monolith of dark stone. Hence I have never been able to persuade anyone to assist me in seizing the treasure, whose hiding place I alone know."

"Why couldn't you do it all by yourself?"

Feng spread his small, long-nailed hands. "I needed a trustworthy assistant to guard my back against any stealthy foe, human or animal, that might approach whilst I was rapt in contemplation of the booty. Moreover, a certain amount of digging and lifting and prying will be required. A gentleman like me lacks the thews for such crude, physical efforts.

"Now harken, gallant sir! This person led the honorable commander through this valley, not by happenstance but by design. When I heard that the Son of Heaven wished me to accompany the brave captain westward, I seized upon the proposal with alacrity. This commission came as a veritable gift from the divine officials in Heaven, for Your Lordship possesses the musculature of three ordinary men. And, being a Western-born foreigner, you naturally do not share the superstitious terrors of us of Kusan. Am I correct in my assumption?"

Conan grunted. "I fear neither god, man, nor devil, and least of all the ghost of a long-dead king. Speak on, Lord Feng."

The duke sidled closer, his voice dropping to a scarcely

audible whisper. "Then, here is my plan. As I have stated, this person guided you hither because I thought you might be he whom I have sought. The task will be light for one of your strength, and my baggage includes tools for excavation. Let us go upon the instant, and within an hour we shall be richer than either of us has dreamed!"

Feng's seductive, purring whisper awoke the lust for loot in Conan's barbaric heart, but a residue of caution restrained the Cimmerian from immediate assent.

"Why not rouse a squad of my troopers to aid us?" he grumbled. "Or your servants? Surely we shall need help in bringing the plunder back to camp!"

Feng shook his sleek head. "Not so, honorable ally! The treasure consists of two small golden caskets of virgin gold, each packed with exceedingly rare and precious gems. We can each carry the fortune of a princedom, and why share this treasure with others? Since the secret is mine alone, I am naturally entitled to half. Then, if you are so lavish as to divide your half amongst your forty warriors . . . well, that is for you to decide."

It took no more urging to persuade Conan to Duke Feng's scheme. The pay of King Yildiz's soldiers was meager and usually in arrears. Conan's recompense for his arduous Turanian service to date had been many empty words of honor and precious little hard coin.

"I go to fetch the digging implements," murmured Feng. "We should leave the camp separately, so as not to arouse suspicion. Whilst I unpack the utensils, you shall don your coat of mail and your arms."

Conan frowned. "Why should I need armor, just to dig up a chest?"

"Oh, excellent sir! There are many dangers in these hills. Here roam the terrible tiger, the fierce leopard, the churlish bear, and the irascible wild bull, not to mention wandering bands of primitive hunters. Since a Khitan gentleman is not trained in the use of arms, your mighty self must be prepared to fight for two. Believe me, noble captain, I know whereof I speak!"

"Oh, all right," grumbled Conan.

"Excellent! I knew that so superior a mind as yours would see the force of my arguments. And now we part, to meet again at the foot of the valley at moonrise. That should occur about one double hour hence, which will give us ample time for our rendezvous."

3.

The night grew darker and the wind, colder. All the eery premonitions of danger, which Conan had experienced since first entering this forsaken vale at sundown, returned in full force. As he walked silently beside the diminutive Khitan, he cast wary glances into the darkness. The steep rock walls on either side narrowed until there was hardly room to walk between the cliffside and the banks of the stream which gurgled out of the valley at their feet.

Behind them, a glow appeared in the misty sky where the heads of the cliffs thrust blackly up against the firmament. This glow grew stronger and became a pearly opalescence. The walls of the valley fell away on either hand, and the two men found themselves treading a grassy sward that spread out on both sides. The stream angled off to the right and, gurgling, curved out of sight between banks clustered with ferns.

As they issued from the valley, the half moon rose over the cliffs behind them. In the misty air, it looked as if the viewer were seeing it from under water. The wan, illusive light of this moon shone upon a small, rounded hill, which rose out of the sward directly before them. Beyond it, steep-sided, forest-crested hills stood up blackly in the watery moonlight.

As the moon cast a powdering of silver over the hill before them, Conan forgot his premonitions. For here rose the monolith of which Feng had spoken. It was a smooth, dully glistening shaft of dark stone, which rose from the top of the hill and soared up until it pierced the layer of mist that overhung the land. The top of the shaft appeared as a mere blur.

Here, then, was the tomb of the long-dead King Hsia, just as Feng had foretold. The treasure must be buried either directly beneath it or to one side. They would soon find out which.

With Feng's crowbar and shovel on his shoulder, Conan pushed forcefully through a clump of tough, elastic rhododendron bushes and started up the hill. He paused to give his small companion a hand up. After a brief scramble, they gained the top of the slope.

Before them, the shaft rose from the center of the gently convex surface of the hilltop. The hill, thought Conan, was probably an artificial mound, such as were sometimes piled up over the remains of great chiefs in his own country. If the treasure were at the bottom of such a pile, it would take more than one night's digging to uncover it . . .

With a startled oath, Conan clutched at his shovel and crowbar. Some invisible force had seized upon them and pulled them toward the shaft. He leaned away from the shaft, his powerful muscles bulging under his mail shirt. Inch by inch, however, the force dragged him toward the monolith. When he saw that he would be drawn against the shaft willy-nilly, he let go of the tools, which flew to the stone. They struck it with a loud double clank and stuck fast to it.

But releasing the tools did not free Conan from the attraction of the monument, which now pulled on his mail shirt as powerfully as it had on the shovel and the crowbar. Staggering and cursing, Conan was slammed

23

against the monolith with crushing force. His back was pinned to the shaft, as were his upper arms where the short sleeves of the mail shirt covered them. So was his head inside the spired Turanian helmet, and so was the scabbarded sword at his waist.

Conan struggled to tear himself free but found that he could not. It was as if unseen chains bound him securely to the column of dark stone.

"What devil's trick is this, you treacherous dog?" he ground out.

Smiling and imperturbable, Feng strolled up to where Conan stood pinned against the pillar. Seemingly impervious to the mysterious force, the Khitan took a silken scarf from one of the baggy sleeves of his silken coat. He waited until Conan opened his mouth to bellow for help, then adroitly jammed a bunch of the silk into Conan's mouth. While Conan gagged and chewed on the cloth, the little man knotted the scarf securely around Conan's head. At last Conan stood, panting but silent, glaring venomously down into the courteous smile of the little duke.

"Forgive the ruse, O noble savage!" lisped Feng. "It was needful that this person concoct some tale to appeal to your primitive lust for gold, in order to allure you hither alone."

Conan's eyes blazed with volcanic fury as he hurled all the might of his powerful body against the invisible bonds that held him against the monolith. It did no good; he was helpless. Sweat trickled down his brow and soaked the cotton haqueton beneath his mail. He tried to shout, but only grunts and gurgles came forth.

"Since, my dear captain, your life approaches its predestined end," continued Feng, "it would be impolite of me not to explain my actions, so that your lowly spirit may journey to whatever hell the gods of the barbarians have prepared for it in full knowledge of the causes of your downfall. Know that the court of his amiable but foolish highness, the king of Kusan, is divided between two parties. One of these, that of the White Peacock, welcomes contact with the barbarians of the West. The other, that of the Golden Pheasant, abominates all association with those animals; and I, of course, am one of the selfless patriots of the Golden Pheasant. Willingly would I give my life to bring your so-called embassy to destruction, lest contact with your barbarous masters contaminate our pure culture and upset our divinely ordained social system.

"Happily, such an extreme measure seems unnecessary. For I have you, the leader of his band of foreign devils, and there around your neck hangs the treaty the Son of Heaven signed with your uncouth heathen king."

The little duke pulled out from under Conan's mail shirt the ivory tube containing the documents. He unclasped the chain that secured it around Conan's neck and tucked it into one of his voluminous sleeves, adding with a malicious smile, "As for the force that holds you prisoner, I will not attempt to explain its subtle nature to your childish wits. Suffice it to explain that the substance whereof this monolith was hewn has the curious property of attracting iron and steel with irresistible force. So fear not; it is no unholy magic that holds you captive."

Conan was little heartened by this news. He had once seen a conjuror in Aghrapur pick up nails with a piece of dark-red stone and supposed that the force that held him was of the same sort. But, since he had never heard of magnetism, it was all equally magic as far as he was concerned.

"Lest you entertain false hopes of rescue by your men," Feng went on, "I have thought of that, also. In these hills dwell the Jagas, a primitive headhunting tribe. Attracted by your campfire, they will assemble at the ends of the valley and rush your camp at dawn. It is their invariable procedure.

"By that time I shall, I hope, be far away. If they capture me, too—well, a man must die some time, and I trust I shall do so with the dignity and decorum befitting one of my rank and culture. My head would make a delightful ornament in a Jaga hut, I am sure.

"And so, my good barbarian, farewell. You will forgive this person for turning his back upon you during your last moments. For your demise is a pity in a way, and I should not enjoy witnessing it. Had you had the advantages of a Khitan upbringing, you would have made an admirable servant—say, a bodyguard for me. But things are as they are."

After a mocking bow of farewell, the Khitan withdrew to the lower slope of the hill. Conan wondered if the Duke's plan was to leave him trapped against the shaft until he perished of starvation and thirst. If his men marked his absence before dawn, they might look for him. But then, since he had stolen out of the camp without leaving word of his going, they would not know whether to be alarmed by his absence. If he could only get word to them, they would scour the countryside for him and make short work of the treacherous little duke. But how to get word?

Again he threw his massive strength against the force that held him crushed against the column, but to no avail. He could move his lower legs and arms and even turn his head somewhat from side to side. But his body was firmly gripped by the iron mail that clothed it.

Now the moon brightened. Conan observed that, about his feet and elsewhere around the base of the monument, grisly remains of other victims were scattered. Human bones and teeth were heaped like old rubbish; he must have trodden upon them when the mysterious force pulled him up against the shaft.

In the stronger light, Conan was disquieted to see that these remains were peculiarly discolored. A closer look showed that the bones seemed to have been eaten away here and there, as if some corrosive fluid had dissolved their smooth surfaces to expose the spongy structure beneath.

He turned his head from side to side, seeking some means of escape. The words of the smooth-tongued Khitan seemed to be true, but now he could discern pieces of iron held against the curiously stained and discolored stone of the column by the invisible force. To his left he sighted the shovel, the crowbar, and the rusty bowl of a helmet, while on the other side a time-eaten dagger was stuck against the stone. Yet once more he hurled his strength against this impalpable force . . .

From below sounded an eery piping sound—a mocking, maddening tune. Straining his eyes through the fickle moonlight, Conan saw that Feng had not left the scene after all. Instead, the duke was sitting on the grass on the side of the hill, near its base. He had drawn a curious flute from his capacious garments and was playing upon it.

Through the shrill piping, a faint, squashy sound reached Conan's ears. It seemed to come from above. The muscles of Conan's bullneck stood out as he twisted his head to look upward; the spired Turanian helmet grated against the stone as he moved. Then the blood froze in his veins.

The mist that had obscured the top of the pylon was gone. The rising half moon shone on and through an amorphous thing, which squatted obscenely on the summit of the column. It was like a huge lump of quivering, semitranslucent jelly—and it lived. Life—throbbing,

27

bloated life—pulsed within it. The moonlight glistened wetly upon it as it beat like a huge, living heart.

4.

As Conan, frozen with horror, watched, the dweller on the top of the monolith sent a trickle of jelly groping down the shaft toward him. The slippery pseudopod slithered over the smooth surface of the stone. Conan began to understand the source of the stains that discolored the face of the monolith.

The wind had changed, and a vagrant down-draft wafted a sickening stench to Conan's nostrils. Now he knew why the bones at the base of the shaft bore that oddly eaten appearance. With a dread that almost unmanned him, he understood that the jellylike thing exuded a digestive fluid, by means of which it consumed its prey. He wondered how many men, in ages past, had stood in his place, bound helplessly to the pillar and awaiting the searing caress of the abomination now descending toward him.

Perhaps Feng's weird piping summoned it, or perhaps the odor of living flesh called it to feast. Whatever the cause, it had begun a slow, inching progress down the side of the shaft toward his face. The wet jelly sucked and slobbered as it slithered slowly toward him.

Despair gave new strength to his cramped, tired muscles. He threw himself from side to side, striving with every last ounce of strength to break the grip of the mysterious force. To his surprise, he found that, in one of his lunges, he slid to one side, partway around the column.

So the grip that held him did not forbid all movement! This gave him food for thought, though he knew that he could not long thus elude the monster of living jelly.

Something prodded his mailed side. Looking down, he saw the rust-eaten dagger he had glimpsed before. His movement sideways had brought the hilt of the weapon against his ribs.

His upper arm was still clamped against the stone by the sleeve of his mail shirt, but his forearm and hand were free. Could he bend his arm far enough to clasp the haft of the dagger?

He strained, inching his hand along the stone. The mail of his arm scraped slowly over the surface; sweat trickled into his eyes. Bit by bit, his straining arm moved toward the handle of the dagger. The taunting tune of Feng's flute sang maddeningly in his ears, while the ungodly stench of the slime-thing filled his nostrils.

His hand touched the dagger, and in an instant he held the hilt fast. But, as he strained it away from the shaft, the rust-eaten blade broke with a sharp *ping*. Rolling his eyes downward, he saw that about two thirds of the blade, from the tapering point back, had broken off and lay flat against the stone. The remaining third still projected from the hilt. Since there was now less iron in the dagger for the shaft to attract, Conan was able, by a muscle-bulging effort, to tear the stump of the weapon away from the shaft.

A glance showed him that, although most of the blade was lost to him, the stump still had a couple of apparently sharp edges. With his muscles quivering from the effort of holding the implement away from the stone, he brought one of these edges up against the leathern thong that bound the two halves of the mail shirt together. Carefully, he began to saw the tough rawhide with the rusty blade.

Every movement was agony. The torment of suspense grew unbearable. His hand, bent into an uncomfortable, twisted position, ached and grew numb. The ancient blade was notched, thin, and brittle; a hasty motion

29

might break it, leaving him helpless. Stroke after stroke he sawed up and down, with exquisite caution. The stench of the creature grew stronger and the sucking sounds of its progress, louder.

Then Conan felt the thong snap. The next instant, he hurled his full strength against the magnetic force that imprisoned him. The thong unraveled through the loopholes in the mail shirt, until one whole side of the shirt was open. His shoulder and half an arm came out through the opening.

Then he felt a light blow on the head. The stench became overpowering, and his unseen assailant from above pushed this way and that against his helmet. Conan knew that a jellylike tendril had reached his helmet and was groping over its surface, seeking flesh. Any instant, the corrosive stuff would seep down over his face . . .

Frantically, he pulled his arm out of the sleeve of the unlaced side of the mail shirt. With his free hand, he unbuckled his sword belt and the chin strap of his helmet. Then he tore himself loose altogether from the deadly constriction of the mail, leaving his tulwar and his armor flattened against the stone.

He staggered free of the column and stood for an instant on trembling legs. The moonlit world swam before his eyes.

Glancing back, he saw that the jelly-beast had now engulfed his helmet. Baffled in its quest for flesh, it was sending more pseudopods down and outward, wavering and questing in the watery light.

Down the slope, the demoniac piping continued. Feng sat cross-legged on the grass of the slope, tweedling away on his flute as if absorbed in some inhuman ecstasy.

Conan ripped off and threw away the gag. He pounced like a striking leopard. He came down, clutching hands first, upon the little duke; the pair rolled down the rest of the slope in a tangle of silken robe and thrashing limbs. A blow to the side of the head subdued Feng's struggles. Conan groped into the Khitan's wide sleeves and tore out the ivory cylinder containing the documents.

Then Conan lurched back up the hill, dragging Feng after him. As he reached the level section around the base of the monolith, he heaved Feng into the air over his head. Seeing what was happening to him, the duke uttered one high, thin scream as Conan hurled him at the shaft. The Khitan struck the column with a thud and slid unconscious to the ground at its base.

The blow was merciful, for the duke never felt the slimy touch of the haunter of the monolith as the glassy tentacles reached his face. For a moment, Conan grimly watched. Feng's features blurred as the rippling jelly slid over them. Then the flesh faded away, and the skull and teeth showed through in a ghastly grin. The abomination flushed pink as it fed.

5.

Conan strode back to camp on stiff legs. Behind him, like a giant's torch, the monolith stood against the sky, wrapped in smoky, scarlet flames.

It had been the work of moments only to strike fire into dry tinder with his flint and steel. He had watched with grim satisfaction as the oily surface of the slime-monster ignited and blazed as it squirmed in voiceless agony. Let them both burn, he thought: the half-digested corpse of that treacherous dog and his loathsome pet!

As Conan neared the camp, he saw that the last of his warriors had not yet retired. Instead, several stood staring curiously at the distant firelight. As he appeared, they turned upon him, crying out: "Where have you been, Captain? What is that blaze? Where is the duke?"

31

"Ho, you gaping oafs!" he roared as he strode into the firelight. "Wake the boys and saddle up to run for it. The Jaga headhunters caught us, and they'll be here any time. They got the duke, but I broke free. Khusro! Mulai! Hop to it, if you do not want your heads hung up in their devil-devil huts! And I hope to Crom you've left me some of that wine!"

The Bloodstained God

Conan continues his service as a soldier of Turan for a total period of about two years, traveling widely and learning the elements of organized warfare. As usual, trouble is his bedfellow. After one of his more unruly episodes—said to have involved the mistress of the commander of the cavalry division in which he was serving—Conan finds it expedient to desert from the Turanian army. Rumors of treasure send him seeking for loot in the Kezankian Mountains, along the eastern borders of Zamora.

IT WAS DARK as the Pit in that stinking alley down which Conan of Cimmeria groped on a quest as blind as the darkness around him. Had there been anyone to witness, they would have seen a tall and enormously powerful man clad in a flowing Zuagir khilat, over that a mail shirt of fine steel mesh, and over that a Zuagir cloak of camel's hair. His mane of black hair and his broad, somber, youthful face, bronzed by the desert sun, were hidden by the Zuagir kaffia.

A sharp, pain-edged cry smote his ears.

Such cries were not uncommon in the twisting alleys of Arenjun, the City of Thieves, and no cautious or timid man would think of interfering in an affair that was none of his business. But Conan was neither cautious nor timid. His ever-lively curiosity would not let him pass by a cry for help; besides, he was searching for certain men, and the disturbance might be a clue to their whereabouts.

Obeying his quick barbarian instincts, he turned toward a beam of light that lanced the darkness close at hand. An instant later he peered through a crack in the close-drawn shutters of a window in a thick stone wall.

He was looking into a spacious room hung with velvet tapestries and littered with costly rugs and couches. About one of these couches a group of men clustered—six brawny Zamorian bravos and two more who eluded identification. On that couch another man was stretched out, a Kezankian tribesman naked to the waist. Though he was a powerful man, a ruffian as muscular as himself gripped each wrist and ankle. Between the four of them they had him spread-eagled on the couch, unable to move, though the muscles stood out in quivering knots on his limbs and shoulders. His eyes gleamed redly and his broad chest glistened with sweat. As Conan looked, a supple man in a turban of red silk lifted a glowing coal from a smoking brazier with a pair of tongs and poised it over the quivering breast, already scarred from similar torture.

Another man, taller than the one with the red turban, snarled a question Conan could not understand. The Kezankian shook his head violently and spat savagely at the questioner. The red-hot coal dropped full on the hairy breast, wrenching an inhuman bellow from the sufferer. In that instant Conan launched his full weight against the shutters.

The Cimmerian's action was not so impulsive as it looked. For his present purposes he needed a friend among the hillmen of the Kezankian range, a people notoriously hostile to all strangers. And here was a chance to get one. The shutters splintered inward with a crash, and he hit the floor inside feet-first, scimitar in one hand and Zuagir sword-knife in the other. The torturers whirled and yelped in astonishment.

They saw a tall, massive figure clad in the garments of a Zuagir, with a fold of his flowing kaffia drawn about his face. Over his mask his eyes blazed a volcanic blue. For an instant the scene held, frozen, then melted into ferocious action.

The man in the red turban snapped a quick word, and a hairy giant lunged to meet the oncoming intruder. The Zamorian held a three-foot sword low, and as he charged he ripped murderously upward. But the down-lashing scimitar met the rising wrist. The hand, still gripping the knife, flew from that wrist in a shower of blood, and the long narrow blade in Conan's left hand sliced through the man's throat, choking the grunt of agony.

Over the crumpling corpse the Cimmerian leaped at Red Turban and his tall companion. Red Turban drew a knife, the tall man a saber.

"Cut him down, Jillad!" snarled Red Turban, retreating before the Cimmerian's impetuous onslaught. "Zal, help here!"

The man called Jillad parried Conan's slash and cut back. Conan avoided the swipe with a shift that would have shamed the leap of a starving panther, and the same movement brought him within reach of Red Turban's knife. The knife shot out; the point struck Conan's side but failed to pierce the shirt of black ring mail. Red Turban leaped back, so narrowly avoiding Conan's knife that the lean blade slit his silken vest and the skin beneath. He tripped over a stool and fell sprawling, but before Conan could follow up his advantage, Jillad was pressing him, raining blows with his saber.

As he parried, the Cimmerian saw that the man called Zal was advancing with a heavy poleax, while Red Turban was scrambling to his feet.

Conan did not wait to be surrounded. A swipe of his scimitar drove Jillad back on his heels. Then, as Zal raised the poleax, Conan darted in under the blow, and the next instant Zal was down, writhing in his own blood and entrails. Conan leaped for the men who still gripped

35

the prisoner. They let go of the man, shouting and drawing their tulwars. One struck at the Kezankian, who evaded the blow by rolling off the bench. Then Conan was between him and them. He retreated before their blows, snarling at the Kezankian:

"Get out! Ahead of me! Quickly!"

"Dogs!" screamed Red Turban. "Don't let them escape!"

"Come and taste of death yourself, dog!" Conan laughed wildly, speaking Zamorian with a barbarous accent.

The Kezankian, weak from torture, slid back a bolt and threw open a door giving upon a small court. He stumbled across the court while behind him Conan faced his tormentors in the doorway, where in the confined space their very numbers hindered them. He laughed and cursed them as he parried and thrust. Red Turban was dancing behind the mob, shrieking curses. Conan's scimitar licked out like the tongue of a cobra, and a Zamorian shrieked and fell, clutching his belly. Jillad, lunging, tripped over him and fell. Before the cursing, squirming figures that jammed the doorway could untangle themselves, Conan turned and ran across the yard toward a wall over which the Kezankian had already disappeared.

Sheathing his weapons, Conan leaped and caught the coping, swung himself up, and had one glimpse of the black, winding street outside. Then something smashed against his head, and limply he toppled from the wall into the shadowy street below.

The tiny glow of a taper in his face roused Conan. He sat up, blinking and cursing, and groped for his sword. Then the light was blown out and a voice spoke in the darkness:

"Be at ease, Conan of Cimmeria. I am your friend."

"Who in Crom's name are you?" demanded Conan. He

36

had found his scimitar on the ground nearby, and he stealthily gathered his legs under him for a spring. He was in the street at the foot of the wall from which he had fallen, and the other man was but a dim bulk looming over him in the shadowy starlight.

"Your friend," repeated the other in a soft Iranistanian accent. "Call me Sassan."

Conan rose, scimitar in hand. The Iranistani extended something toward him. Conan caught the glint of steel in the starlight, but before he could strike he saw that it was his own knife, hilt first.

"You're as suspicious as a starving wolf, Conan," laughed Sassan. "But save your steel for your enemies."

"Where are they?" Conan took the knife.

"Gone. Into the mountains, on the trail of the blood-stained god."

Conan started and caught Sassan's khilat in an iron grip and glared into the man's dark eyes, mocking and mysterious in the starlight.

"Damn you, what know you of the bloodstained god?" Conan's knife touched the Iranistani's side below his ribs.

"I know this," said Sassan. "You came to Arenjun following thieves who stole from you the map of a treasure greater than Yildiz's hoard. I, too, came seeking something. I was hiding nearby, watching through a hole in the wall, when you burst into the room where the Kezankian was being tortured. How did you know it was they who stole your map?"

"I didn't," muttered Conan. "I heard a man cry out and thought it a good idea to interfere. If I had known they were the men I sought . . . how much do you know?"

"This much. Hidden in the mountains near here is an ancient temple which the hill folk fear to enter. It is said to go back to Pre-Cataclysmic times, though the wise men disagree as to whether it is Grondarian or was built by the unknown pre-human folk who ruled the Hyrkanians just after the Cataclysm.

"The Kezankians forbid the region to all outsiders, but a Nemedian named Ostorio did find the temple. He entered it and discovered a golden idol crusted with red jewels, which he called the bloodstained god. He could not bring it away with him, as it was bigger than a man, but he made a map, intending to return. Although he got safely away, he was stabbed by some ruffian in Shadizar and died there. Before he died he gave the map to you, Conan."

"Well?" demanded Conan grimly. The house behind him was dark and still.

"The map was stolen," said Sassan. "By whom, you know."

"I didn't know at the time," growled Conan. "Later I learned the thieves were Zyras, a Corinthian, and Arshak, a disinherited Turanian prince. Some skulking servant spied on Ostorio as he lay dying and told them. Though I knew neither by sight, I traced them to this city. Tonight I learned they were hiding in this alley. I was blundering about looking for a clue when I stumbled into that brawl."

"You fought them in ignorance!" said Sassan. "The Kezankian was Rustum, a spy of the Kezankian chieftain Keraspa. They lured him into their house and were singeing him to make him tell them of the secret trails through the mountains. You know the rest."

"All except what happened when I climbed the wall."

"Somebody threw a stool at you and hit your head. When you fell outside the wall they paid you no more heed. either thinking you were dead or not knowing you in your mask. They chased the Kezankian, but whether they caught him I know not. Soon they returned, saddled up, and rode like madmen westward, leaving the dead where they fell. I came to see who you were and recognized you."

"Then the man in the red turban was Arshak," muttered Conan. "But where was Zyras?"

"Disguised as a Turanian—the man they called Jillad."

"Oh. Well then?" growled Conan.

"Like you, I want the red god, even though of all the men who have sought it down the centuries only Ostorio escaped with his life. There is supposed to be some mysterious curse on would-be plunderers—"

"What know you of that?" said Conan, sharply.

Sassan shrugged. "Nothing much. The folk of Kezankia speak of a doom that the god inflicts on those who raise covetous hands against him, but I'm no superstitious fool. You're not afraid, are you?"

"Of course not!" As a matter of fact Conan was. Though he feared no man or beast, the supernatural filled his barbarian's mind with atavistic terrors. Still, he did not care to admit the fact. "What have you in mind?"

"Why, only that neither of us can fight Zyras' whole band alone, but together we can follow them and take the idol from them. What do you say?"

"Aye, I'll do it. But I'll kill you like a dog if you try any tricks!"

Sassan laughed. "I know you would, so you can trust me. Come; I have horses waiting."

The Iranistani led the way through twisting streets overhung with latticed balconies and along stinking alleys until he stopped at the lamplit door of a courtyard. At his knock, a bearded face appeared at the wicket. After some muttered words, the gate opened. Sassan strode in, Conan following suspiciously. But the horses were there, and a word from the keeper of the serai set sleepy servants to saddling them and filling the saddle pouches with food.

Soon Conan and Sassan were riding together out of

the west gate, perfunctorily challenged by the sleepy guard. Sassan was portly but muscular, with a broad, shrewd face and dark, alert eyes. He bore a horseman's lance over his shoulder and handled his weapons with the expertness of practice. Conan did not doubt that in a pinch he would fight with cunning and courage. Conan also did not doubt that he could trust Sassan to play fair just so long as the alliance was to his advantage, and to murder his partner at the first opportunity when it became expedient to do so in order to keep all the treasure himself.

Dawn found them riding through the rugged defiles of the bare, brown, rocky Kezankian Mountains, separating the easternmost marches of Koth and Zamora from the Turanian steppes. Though both Koth and Zamora claimed the region, neither had been able to subdue it, and the town of Arenjun, perched on a steep-sided hill, had successfully withstood two sieges by the Turanian hordes from the east. The road branched and became fainter until Sassan confessed himself at a loss to know where they were.

"I'm still following their tracks," grunted Conan. "If you cannot see them, I can."

Hours passed, and signs of the recent passage of horses became clear. Conan said: "We're closing on them, and they still outnumber us. Let us stay out of sight until they get the idol, then ambush them and take it from them."

Sassan's eyes gleamed. "Good! But let's be wary; this is the country of Keraspa, who robs all he catches."

Midafternoon found them still following the trace of an ancient, forgotten road. As they rode toward a narrow gorge, Sassan said:

"If that Kezankian got back to Keraspa, the Kezankians will be alert for strangers . . ."

They reined up as a lean, hawk-faced Kezankian rode out of the gorge with hand upraised. "Halt!" he cried. "By what leave do you ride in the land of Keraspa?"

"Careful," muttered Conan. "They may be all around us."

"Keraspa claims toll on travelers," answered Sassan under his breath. "Maybe that is all this fellow wants." Fumbling in his girdle, he said to the tribesman: "We are but poor travelers, glad to pay your brave chief's toll. We ride alone."

"Then who is that behind you?" demanded the Kezankian, nodding his head in the direction from which they had come.

Sassan half turned his head. Instantly the Kezankian whipped a dagger from his girdle and struck at the Iranistani.

Quick as he was, Conan was quicker. As the dagger darted at Sassan's throat, Conan's scimitar flashed and steel rang. The dagger whirled away, and with a snarl the Kezankian caught at his sword. Before he could pull the blade free, Conan struck again, cleaving turban and skull. The Kezankian's horse neighed and reared, throwing the corpse headlong. Conan wrenched his own steed around.

"Ride for the gorge!" he yelled. "It's an ambush!"

As the Kezankian tumbled to earth, there came the flat snap of bows and the whistle of arrows. Sassan's horse leaped as an arrow struck it in the neck and bolted for the mouth of the defile. Conan felt an arrow tug at his sleeve as he struck in the spurs and fled after Sassan, who was unable to control his beast.

As they swept towards the mouth of the gorge, three horsemen rode out swinging broad-bladed tulwars. Sassan, abandoning his effort to check his maddened mount, drove his lance at the nearest. The spear transfixed the man and hurled him out of the saddle.

The next instant Conan was even with a second swords-

41

man, who swung the heavy tulwar. The Cimmerian threw up his scimitar and the blades met with a crash as the horses came together breast to breast. Conan, rising in his stirrups, smote downwards with all his immense strength, beating down the tulwar and splitting the skull of the wielder. Then he was galloping up the gorge with arrows screeching past him. Sassan's wounded horse stumbled and went down; the Iranistani leaped clear as it fell.

Conan pulled up, snarling: "Get up behind me!" Sassan, lance in hand, leaped up behind the saddle. A touch of the spurs, and the heavily-burdened horse set off down the gorge. Yells behind showed that the tribesmen were scampering to their hidden horses. A turn in the gorge muffled the noises.

"That Kezankian spy must have gotten back to Keraspa," panted Sassan. "They want blood, not gold. Do you suppose they have wiped out Zyras?"

"He might have passed before they set up their ambush, or they might have been following him when they turned to trap us. I think he's still ahead of us."

A mile further on they heard faint sounds of pursuit. Then they came out into a natural bowl walled by sheer cliffs. From the midst of this bowl a slope led up to a bottleneck pass on the other side. As they neared this pass, Conan saw that a low stone wall closed the gut of the pass. Sassan yelled and jumped down from the horse as a flight of arrows screeched past. One struck the horse in the chest.

The beast lurched to a thundering fall, and Conan jumped clear and rolled behind a cluster of rocks, where Sassan had already taken cover. More arrows splintered against boulders or stuck quivering in the earth. The two adventurers looked at each other with sardonic humor.

"We've found Zyras!" said Sassan.

"In an instant," laughed Conan, "they'll rush us, and Keraspa will come up beehind us to close the trap."

42

A taunting voice shouted: "Come out and get shot, curs! Who's the Zuagir with you, Sassan? I thought I had brained him last night!"

"My name is Conan," roared the Cimmerian.

After a moment of silence, Zyras shouted: "I might have known! Well, we have you now!"

"You're in the same fix!" yelled Conan. "You heard the fighting back down the gorge?"

"Aye; we heard it when we stopped to water the horses. Who's chasing you?"

"Keraspa and a hundred Kezankians! When we are dead, do you think he'll let you go after you tortured one of his men?"

"You had better let us join you," added Sassan.

"Is that the truth?" yelled Zyras, his turbaned head appearing over the wall.

"Are you deaf, man?" retorted Conan.

The gorge reverberated with yells and hoofbeats.

"Get in, quickly!" shouted Zyras. "Time enough to divide the idol if we get out of this alive."

Conan and Sassan leaped up and ran up the slope to the wall, where hairy arms helped them over. Conan looked at his new allies: Zyras, grim and hard-eyed in his Turanian guise; Arshak, still dapper after leagues of riding, and three swarthy Zamorians who bared their teeth in greeting. Zyras and Arshak each wore a shirt of chain mail like those of Conan and Sassan.

The Kezankians, about a score of them, reined up as the bows of the Zamorians and Arshak sent arrows swishing among them. Some of them shot back; others whirled and rode back out of range to dismount, as the wall was too high to be carried by a mounted charge. One saddle was emptied and one wounded horse bolted back down the gorge with its rider.

"They must have been following us," snarled Zyras. "Conan, you lied! That is no hundred men!"

43

"Enough to cut our throats," said Conan, trying his sword. "And Keraspa can send for reinforcements whenever he likes."

Zyras growled: "We have a chance behind this wall. I believe it was built by the same race that built the red god's temple. Save your arrows for the rush."

Covered by a continuous discharge of arrows from four of their number on the flanks, the rest of the Kezankians ran up the slope in a solid mass, those in front holding up light bucklers. Behind them Conan saw Keraspa's red beard as the wily chief urged his men on.

"Shoot!" screamed Zyras. Arrows plunged into the mass of men and three writhing figures were left behind on the slope, but the rest came on, eyes glaring and blades glittering in hairy fists.

The defenders shot their last arrows into the mass and then rose up behind the wall, drawing steel. The mountaineers rolled up against the wall. Some tried to boost their fellows up to the top; others pushed small boulders up against the foot of the wall to provide steps. Along the barrier sounded the smash of bone-breaking blows, the rasp and slither of steel, the gasping oaths of dying men. Conan hewed the head from the body of a Kezankian, and beside him saw Sassan thrust his spear into the open mouth of another until the point came out the back of the man's neck. A wild-eyed tribesman stabbed a long knife into the belly of one of the Zamorians. Into the gap left by the falling body the howling Kezankian lunged, hurling himself up and over the wall before Conan could stop him. The giant Cimmerian took a cut on his left arm and crushed in the man's shoulder with a return blow.

Leaping over the body, he hewed into the men swarming up over the wall with no time to see how the fight was going on either side. Zyras was cursing in Corinthian and Arshak in Hyrkanian. Somebody screamed in mortal

44

agony. A tribesman got a pair of gorilla-like hands on Conan's thick neck, but the Cimmerian tensed his neck muscles and stabbed low with his knife again and again until with a moan the Kezankian released him and toppled from the wall.

Gasping for air, Conan looked about him, realizing that the pressure had slackened. The few remaining Kezankians were staggering down the slope, all streaming blood. Corpses lay piled deep at the foot of the wall. All three of the Zamorians were dead or dying, and Conan saw Arshak sitting with his back against the wall, his hands pressed to his body while blood seeped between his fingers. The prince's lips were blue, but he achieved a ghastly smile.

"Born in a palace," he whispered, "and dying behind a rock wall! No matter—it is fate. There is a curse on the treasure—all men who rode on the trail of the blood stained god have died . . ." And he died.

Zyras, Conan, and Sassan glanced silently at one another: three grim tattered figures, all splashed with blood. All had taken minor wounds on their limbs, but their mail shirts had saved them from the death that had befallen their companions.

"I saw Keraspa sneaking off!" snarled Zyras. "He'll make for his village and get the whole tribe on our trail. Let us make a race of it: get the idol and drag it out of the mountains before he catches us. There's enough treasure for all."

"True," growled Conan. "But give me back my map before we start."

Zyras opened his mouth to speak, and then saw that Sassan had picked up one of the Zamorians' bows and had drawn an arrow on him. "Do as Conan tells you," said the Iranistani.

Zyras shrugged and handed over a crumpled parchment. "Curse you, I still deserve a third of the treasure!"

45

Conan glanced at the map and thrust it into his girdle. "All right; I'll not hold a grudge. You're a swine, but if you play fair with us we'll do the same, eh, Sassan?"

Sassan nodded and gathered up a quiverful of arrows.

The horses of Zyras' party were tied in the pass behind the wall. The three men mounted the best beasts and led the three others, up the canyon behind the pass. Night fell, but with Keraspa behind them they pushed recklessly on.

Conan watched his companions like a hawk. The most dangerous time would come when they had secured the golden statue and no longer needed each other's help. Then Zyras and Sassan might conspire to murder Conan, or one of them might approach him with a plan to slay the third man. Tough and ruthless though the Cimmerian was, his barbaric code of honor would not let him be the first to try treachery.

He also wondered what it was that the maker of the map had tried to tell him just before he died. Death had come upon Ostorio in the midst of a description of the temple, with a gush of blood from his mouth. The Nemedian had been about to warn him of something, he thought—but of what?

Dawn broke as they came out of a narrow gorge into a steep-walled valley. The defile through which they had entered was the only way in. It came out upon a ledge thirty paces wide, with the cliff rising a bowshot above it on one side and falling away to an unmeasurable depth below. There seemed no way down into the mist-veiled depths of the valley far below. The men wasted few glances in this direction, for the sight ahead drove hunger and fatigue from their minds.

There on the ledge stood the temple, gleaming in the rising sun. It was carved out of the sheer rock of the cliff, its great portico facing them. The ledge led to its great bronzen door, green with age.

What race or culture it represented Conan did not try to guess. He unfolded the map and glanced at the notes on the margin, trying to discover a method of opening the door.

But Sassan slipped from his saddle and ran ahead of them, crying out in his greed.

"Fool!" grunted Zyras, swinging down from his horse. "Ostorio left a warning on the margin of the map; something about the god's taking his toll."

Sassan was pulling at the various ornaments and projections on the portal. They heard him cry out in triumph as it moved under his hands. Then his cry changed to a scream as the door, a ton of bronze, swayed outward and fell crashing, squashing the Iranistani like an insect. He was completely hidden by the great metal slab, from beneath which oozed streams of crimson.

Zyras shrugged. "I said he was a fool. Ostorio must have found some way to swing the door without releasing it from its hinges."

One less knife in the back to watch for, thought Conan. "Those hinges are false," he said, examining the mechanism at close range. "Ho! The door is rising back up again!"

The hinges were, as Conan had said, fakes. The door was actually mounted on a pair of swivels at the lower corners so that it could fall outward like a drawbridge. From each upper corner of the door a chain ran diagonally up, to disappear into a hole near the upper corner of the door-frame. Now, with a distant grinding sound, the chains had tautened and had started to pull the door back up into its former position.

Conan snatched up the lance that Sassan had dropped. Placing the butt in a hollow in the carvings of the inner

47

surface of the door, he wedged the point into the corner of the door frame. The grinding sound ceased and the door stopped moving in a nine-tenths open position.

"That was clever, Conan," said Zyras. "As the god has now had his toll, the way should be open."

He stepped up on to the inner surface of the door and strode into the temple. Conan followed. They paused on the threshold and peered into the shadowy interior as they might have peered into a serpent's lair. Silence held the ancient temple, broken only by the soft scuff of their boots.

They entered cautiously, blinking in the half-gloom. In the dimness, a blaze of crimson like the glow of a sunset smote their eyes. They saw the god, a thing of gold crusted with flaming gems.

The statue, a little bigger than life size, was in the form of a dwarfish man standing upright on great splay feet on a block of basalt. The statue faced the entrance, and on each side of it stood a great carven chair of dense black wood, inlaid with gems and mother-of-pearl in a style unlike that of any living nation.

To the left of the statue, a few feet from the base of the pedestal, the floor of the temple was cleft from wall to wall by a chasm some fifteen feet wide. At some time, probably before the temple had been built, an earthquake had split the rock. Into that black abyss, ages ago, screaming victims had doubtless been hurled by hideous priests as sacrifices to the god. The walls were lofty and fantastically carved, the roof dim and shadowy above.

But the attention of the men was fixed on the idol. Though a brutish and repellant monstrosity, it represented wealth that made Conan's brain swim.

"Crom and Ymir!" breathed Conan. "One could buy a kingdom with those rubies!"

"Too much to share with a lout of a barbarian," panted Zyras.

These words, spoken half-unconsciously between the Corinthian's clenched teeth, warned Conan. He ducked just as Zyras' sword whistled towards his neck; the blade sliced a fold from his headdress. Cursing his own carelessness, Conan leaped back and drew his scimitar.

Zyras came on in a rush and Conan met him. Back and forth they fought before the leering idol, feet scuffing on the rock, blades rasping and ringing. Conan was larger than the Corinthian, but Zyras was strong, agile, and experienced, full of deadly tricks. Again and again Conan dodged death by a hair's breadth.

Then Conan's foot slipped on the smooth floor and his blade wavered. Zyras threw all his strength and speed into a lunge that would have driven his saber through Conan. But the Cimmerian was not so off balance as he looked. With the suppleness of a panther, he twisted his powerful body aside so that the long blade passed under his right armpit, plowing through his loose khilat. For an instant, the blade caught in the cloth. Zyras stabbed with the dagger in his left hand. The blade sank into Conan's right arm, and at the same time the knife in Conan's left drove through Zyras' mail shirt, snapping the links, and plunged between Zyras' ribs. Zyras screamed, gurgled, reeled back, and fell limply.

Conan dropped his weapons and knelt, ripping a strip of cloth from his robe for a bandage, to add to those he already wore. He bound up the wound, tying knots with fingers and teeth, and glanced at the bloodstained god leering down at him. Its gargoyle face seemed to gloat. Conan shivered as the superstitious fears of the barbarian ran down his spine.

Then he braced himself. The red god was his, but the problem was, how to get the thing away? If it were solid it would be much too heavy to move, but a tap of the butt of his knife assured him that it was hollow. He was pacing about, his head full of schemes for knocking one

49

of the carven thrones apart to make a sledge, levering the god off its base, and hauling it out of the temple by means of the extra horses and the chains that worked the falling front door, when a voice made him whirl.

"Stand where you are!" It was a shout of triumph in the Kezankian dialect of Zamoria.

Conan saw two men in the doorway, each aiming at him a heavy double-curved bow of the Hyrkanian type. One was tall, lean, and red-bearded.

"Keraspa!" said Conan, reaching for the sword and the knife he had dropped.

The other man was a powerful fellow who seemed familiar.

"Stand back!" said the Kezankian chief. "You thought I had run away to my village, did you not? Well, I followed you all night, with the only one of my men not wounded." His glance appraised the idol. "Had I known the temple contained such treasure I should have looted it long ago, despite the superstitions of my people. Rustum, pick up his sword and dagger."

The man stared at the brazen hawk's head that formed the pommel of Conan's scimitar.

"Wait!" he cried. "This is he who saved me from torture in Arenjun! I know this blade!"

"Be silent!" snarled the chief. "The thief dies!"

"Nay! He saved my life! What have I ever had from you but hard tasks and scanty pay? I renounce my allegiance, you dog!"

Rustum stepped forward, raising Conan's sword, but then Keraspa turned and released his arrow. The missile thudded into Rustum's body. The tribesman shrieked and staggered back under the impact, across the floor of the temple, and over the edge of the chasm. His screams came up, fainter and fainter, until they could no longer be heard.

Quick as a striking snake, before the unarmed Conan

could spring upon him, Keraspa whipped another arrow from his quiver and nocked it. Conan had taken one step in a tigerish rush that would have thrown him upon the chief anyway when, without the slightest warning, the ruby-crusted god stepped down from its pedestal with a heavy metallic sound and took one long stride towards Keraspa.

With a frightful scream, the chief released his arrow at the animated statue. The arrow struck the god's shoulder and bounced high, turning over and over, and the idol's long arms shot out and caught the chief by an arm and a leg.

Scream after scream came from the foaming lips of Keraspa as the god turned and moved ponderously towards the chasm. The sight had frozen Conan with horror, and now the idol blocked his way to the exit; either to the right or the left his path would take him within reach of one of those ape-long arms. And the god, for all its mass, moved as quickly as a man.

The red god neared the chasm and raised Keraspa high over its head to hurl him into the depths. Conan saw Keraspa's mouth open in the midst of his foam-dabbled beard, shrieking madly. When Keraspa had been disposed of, no doubt the statue would take care of him. The ancient priests did not have to throw the god's victims into the gulf; the image took care of that detail himself.

As the god swayed back on its golden heels to throw the chief, Conan, groping behind him, felt the wood of one of the thrones. These had no doubt been occupied by the high priests or other functionaries of the cult in the ancient days. Conan turned, grasped the massive chair by its back, and lifted it. With muscles cracking under the strain, he whirled the throne over his head and struck the god's golden back between the shoulders, just as Keraspa's body, still screaming, was cast into the abyss.

51

The wood of the throne splintered under the impact with a rending crash. The blow caught the deity moving forward with the impulse that it had given Keraspa and overbalanced it. For the fraction of a second the monstrosity tottered on the edge of the chasm, long golden arms lashing the air; and then it, too, toppled into the gulf.

Conan dropped the remains of the throne to peer over the edge of the abyss. Keraspa's screams had ceased. Conan fancied that he heard a distant sound such as the idol might have made in striking the side of the cliff and bouncing off, far below, but he could not be sure. There was no final crash or thump; only silence.

Conan drew his muscular forearm across his forehead and grinned wryly. The curse of the bloodstained god was ended, and the god with it. For all the wealth that had gone into the chasm with the idol, the Cimmerian was not sorry to have bought his life at that price. And there were other treasures.

He gathered up his sword and Rustum's bow, and went out into the morning sunshine to pick a horse.

The Frost Giant's Daughter

Fed up with civilization and its magic, Conan rides back to his native Cimmeria. After a month or two of wenching and drinking, however, he grows restless enough to join his old friends, the Æsir, in a raid into Vanaheim.

THE CLANGOR of sword and ax had died away; the shouting of the slaughter was hushed; silence lay on the red-stained snow. The bleak, pale sun that glittered so blindingly from the ice fields and the snow-covered plains struck sheens of silver from rent corselet and broken blade where the dead lay as they had fallen. The nerveless hand yet gripped the broken hilt; helmeted heads, drawn back in their death throes, tilted red beards and golden beards grimly upward, as if in a last invocation to Ymir the frost giant, god of a warrior race.

Across the reddened drifts and the mail-clad forms, two figures glared at each other. In all that utter desolation, they alone moved. The frosty sky was over them, the white illimitable plain around them, the dead men at their feet. Slowly through the corpses they came, as ghosts might come to a tryst through the shambles of a dead world. In the brooding silence, they stood face to face.

Both were tall men, built as powerfully as tigers. Their shields were gone, their corselets battered and dented. Blood dried on their mail; their swords were stained red. Their horned helmets showed the marks of fierce strokes.

One was beardless and black-maned; the locks and beard of the other were as red as the blood on the sunlit snow.

"Man," said the latter, "tell me your name, so that my brothers in Vanaheim may know who was the last of Wulfhere's band to fall before the sword of Heimdul."

"Not in Vanaheim," growled the black-haired warrior, "but in Valhalla shall you tell your brothers that you met Conan of Cimmeria!"

Heimdul roared and leaped, his sword flashing in a deadly arc. As the singing blade crashed on his helmet, shivering into bits of blue fire, Conan staggered, and his vision was filled with red sparks. But, as he reeled, he thrust with all the power of his broad shoulders behind the blade. The sharp point tore through brass scales and bones and heart, and the red-haired warrior died at Conan's feet.

The Cimmerian stood upright, trailing his sword, a sudden sick weariness assailing him. The glare of the sun on the snow cut his eyes like a knife, and the sky seemed shrunken and strangely apart. He turned away from the trampled expanse, where yellow-bearded warriors lay locked with red-haired slayers in the embrace of death. A few steps he took, and the glare of the snow fields was suddenly dimmed. A rushing wave of blindness engulfed him, and he sank down into the snow, supporting himself on one mailed arm and seeking to shake the blindness out of his eyes as a lion might shake his mane.

A silvery laugh cut through his dizziness, and his sight slowly cleared. He looked up; there was a strangeness about all the landscape that he could not place or define—an unfamiliar tinge to earth and sky. But he did not think long of this. Before him, swaying like a sapling in the wind, stood a woman. To his dazed eyes her body was like ivory, and, save for a light veil of gossamer, she was naked as the day. Her slender feet were whiter than the snow they spurned. She laughed down at the bewildered warrior with a laughter that was sweeter than the rippling of silvery fountains and poisonous with cruel mockery.

"Who are you?" asked the Cimmerian. "Whence come you?"

"What matter?" Her voice was more musical than a silver-stringed harp, but edged with cruelty.

"Call up your men," said he grasping his sword. "Though my strength fail me, yet they shall not take me alive. I see that you are of the Vanir."

"Have I said so?"

His gaze went again to her unruly locks, which at first glance he had thought to be red. Now he saw that they were neither red nor yellow but a glorious compound of both colors. He gazed spellbound. Her hair was like elfin gold; the sun struck it so dazzlingly that he could scarcely bear to look upon it. Her eyes were likewise neither wholly blue nor wholly gray, but of shifting colors and dancing lights and clouds of colors he could not have named. Her full red lips smiled, and from her slender feet to the blinding crown of her billowy hair, her ivory body was as perfect as the dream of a god. Conan's pulse hammered in his temples.

"I cannot tell," said he, "whether you are of Vanaheim and mine enemy, or of Asgard and my friend. Far have I wandered, but a woman like you I have never seen. Your locks blind me with their brightness. Never have I seen such hair, not even among the fairest daughters of the Æsir. By Ymir—"

"Who are you to swear by Ymir?" she mocked. "What know you of the gods of ice and snow, you who have come up from the South to adventure among an alien people?"

"By the dark gods of my own race!" he cried in anger. "Though I am not of the golden-haired Æsir, none has been more forward in swordplay! This day I have seen fourscore men fall, and I alone have survived the field where Wulfhere's reavers met the wolves of Bragi. Tell me, woman, have you seen the flash of mail out across the snow plains, or seen armed men moving upon the ice?"

"I have seen the hoarfrost glittering in the sun," she answered. "I have heard the wind whispering across the everlasting snows."

He shook his head with a sigh. "Niord should have come up with us before the battle joined. I fear he and his fighting men have been ambushed. Wulfhere and his warriors lie dead . . . I had thought there was no village within many leagues of this spot, for the war carried us far; but you cannot have come a great distance over these snows, naked as you are. Lead me to your tribe, if you are of Asgard, for I am faint with blows and the weariness of strife."

"My village is further than you can walk, Conan of Cimmeria," she laughed. Spreading her arms wide, she swayed before him, her golden head lolling sensuously and her scintillant eyes half shadowed beneath their long silken lashes. "Am I not beautiful, O man?"

"Like dawn running naked on the snows," he muttered, his eyes burning like those of a wolf.

"Then why do you not rise and follow me? Who is the strong warrior who falls down before me?" she chanted in maddening mockery. "Lie down and die in the snow with the other fools, Conan of the black hair. You cannot follow where I would lead."

With an oath, the Cimmerian heaved himself up on his feet, his blue eyes blazing, his dark, scarred face contorted. Rage shook his soul, but desire for the taunting figure before him hammered at his temples and drove his wild blood fiercely through his veins. Passion fierce as physical agony flooded his whole being, so that earth and sky swam red to his dizzy gaze. In the madness that

56

swept upon him, weariness and faintness were swept away.

He spoke no word as he sheathed his bloody sword and drove at her, fingers spread to grip her soft flesh. With a shriek of laughter she leaped back and ran, laughing at him over her white shoulder. With a low growl, Conan followed. He had forgotten the fight, forgotten the mailed warriors who lay in their blood, forgotten Niord and the reavers who failed to reach the battle. He thought only of the slender white shape, which seemed to float rather than run before him.

Out across the blinding-white plain the chase led. The trampled red field fell out of sight behind him, but still Conan kept on with the silent tenacity of his race. His mailed feet broke through the frozen crust; he sank deep in the drifts and forged through them by sheer brute strength. But the girl danced across the snow, light as a feather floating on a pool; her naked feet barely left their imprint on the hoarfrost that overlaid the crust. Despite the fire in his veins, the cold bit through the warrior's mail and fur-lined tunic; but the girl in her gossamer veil ran as lightly and as gaily as if she danced through the palms and rose gardens of Poitain.

On and on she led, and Conan followed. Black curses drooled through the Cimmerian's parched lips. The great veins in his temples swelled and throbbed, and his teeth gnashed.

"You cannot escape me!" he roared. "Lead me into a trap and I'll pile the heads of your kinsmen at your feet! Hide from me and I'll tear the mountains apart to find you! I'll follow you to Hell itself!"

Foam flew from the barbarian's lips as her maddening laughter floated back to him. Farther and farther into the wastes she led him. As the hours passed and the sun slid down its long slant to the horizon, the land changed; the wide plains gave way to low hills, marching upward in broken ranges. Far to the north he caught a glimpse of towering mountains, their eternal snows blue with distance and pink in the rays of the blood-red setting sun. In the darkling skies above them shone the flaring rays of the aurora. They spread fanwise into the sky—frosty blades of cold, flaming light, changing in color, growing and brightening.

Above him the skies glowed and crackled with strange lights and gleams. The snow shone weirdly: now frosty blue, now icy crimson, now cold silver. Through a shimmering, icy realm of enchantment Conan plunged doggedly onward, in a crystalline maze where the only reality was the white body dancing across the glittering snow beyond his reach—ever beyond his reach.

He did not wonder at the strangeness of it all—not even when two gigantic figures rose up to bar his way. The scales of their mail were white with hoarfrost; their helmets and axes were covered with ice. Snow sprinkled their locks, in their beards were spikes of icicles, and their eyes were as cold as the lights that streamed above them.

"Brothers!" cried the girl, dancing between them. "Look who follows! I have brought you a man to slay! Take his heart, that we may lay it smoking on our father's board!"

The giants answered with roars like the grinding of icebergs on a frozen shore. They heaved up their axes, shining in the starlight, as the maddened Cimmerian hurled himself upon them. A frosty blade flashed before his eyes, blinding him with its brightness, and he gave back a terrible stroke that sheared through his foe's leg at the knee.

With a groan, the victim fell, and at the same instant Conan was dashed into the snow, his left shoulder numb from a glancing blow of the survivor's ax, from which the Cimmerian's mail had barely saved his life. Conan saw the remaining giant looming high above him like a colossus carved of ice, etched against the coldly glowing sky. The ax fell—to sink through the snow and deep into the frozen earth as Conan hurled himself aside and leaped to his feet. The giant roared and wrenched his ax free; but, even as he did, Conan's sword sang down. The giant's knees bent, and he sank slowly into the snow, which turned crimson with the blood that gushed from his half-severed neck.

Conan wheeled to see the girl standing a short distance away, staring at him in wide-eyed horror, all the mockery gone from her face. He cried out fiercely, and drops of blood flew from his sword as his hand shook in the intensity of his passion.

"Call the rest of your brothers!" he cried. "I'll give their hearts to the wolves! You cannot escape me . . ."

With a cry of fright, she turned and ran fleetly. She did not laugh now, nor mock him over her white shoulder. She ran as for her life. Although he strained every nerve and thew, until his temples were like to burst and the snow swam red to his gaze, she drew away from him, dwindling in the witch-fire of the skies until she was a figure no bigger than a child, then a dancing white flame on the snow, then a dim blur in the distance. But, grinding his teeth until the blood started from his gums, Conan reeled on, until he saw the blur grow to a dancing white flame, and the flame to a figure as big as a child; and then she was running less than a hundred paces ahead of him. Slowly, foot by foot, the space narrowed.

She was running with effort now, her golden locks blowing free; he heard the quick panting of her breath and saw the flash of fear in the look she cast over her white shoulder. The grim endurance of the barbarian served him well. The speed ebbed from her flashing white legs; she reeled in her gait. In Conan's untamed soul leaped up the fires of Hell she had so well fanned. With an inhuman roar, he closed in on her, just as she wheeled with a haunting cry and flung out her arms to fend him off.

His sword fell into the snow as he crushed her to him. Her lithe body bent backward as she fought with desperate frenzy in his iron arms. Her golden hair blew about his face, blinding him with its sheen; the feel of her slender body, twisting in his mailed arms, drove him to blinder madness. His strong fingers sank deep into her smooth flesh—flesh as cold as ice. It was as if he embraced, not a woman of human flesh and blood, but a woman of flaming ice. She writhed her golden head aside, striving to avoid the fierce kisses that bruised her red lips.

"You are as cold as the snows," he mumbled dazedly. "I'll warm you with the fire of my own blood . . ."

With a scream and a desperate wrench, she slipped from his arms, leaving her single gossamer garment in his grasp. She sprang back and faced him, her golden locks in wild disarray, her white bosom heaving, her beautiful eyes blazing with terror. For an instant he stood frozen, awed by her terrible beauty as she stood naked against the snows.

And in that instant she flung her arms toward the lights that glowed in the skies and cried out, in a voice that would ring in Conan's ears forever after : "Ymir! O my father, save me!"

Conan was leaping forward, arms spread to seize her, when with a crack like the breaking of a mountain of ice the whole sky leaped into icy fire. The girl's ivory body was suddenly enveloped in a cold, blue flame so blinding that the Cimmerian threw up his hands to shield his eyes from the intolerable blaze. For a fleeting instant, skies and snowy hills were bathed in crackling white flames, blue darts of icy light, and frozen crimson fires.

Then Conan staggered and cried out. The girl was gone. The glowing snow lay empty and bare; high above his head the witch-lights played in a frosty sky gone mad.

Among the distant blue mountains there sounded a rolling thunder as of a gigantic war chariot, rushing behind steeds whose frantic hoofs struck lightning from the snows and echoes from the skies.

Then the aurora, the snow-clad hills, and the blazing heavens reeled drunkenly to Conan's sight. Thousands of fireballs burst with showers of sparks, and the sky itself became a titanic wheel, which rained stars as it spun. Under his feet the snowy hills heaved up like a wave, and the Cimmerian crumpled into the snows to lie motionless.

In a cold dark universe, whose sun was extinguished eons ago, Conan felt the movement of life, alien and unguessed. An earthquake had him in its grip and was shaking him to and fro, at the same time chafing his hands and feet until he yelled in pain and fury and groped for his sword.

"He's coming to, Horsa," said a voice. "Hasten—we must rub the frost out of his limbs, if he's ever to wield sword again."

"He won't open his left hand," growled another. "He's clutching something—"

Conan opened his eyes and stared into the bearded faces that bent over him. He was surrounded by tall, golden-haired warriors in mail and furs.

"Conan!" said one. "You live!"

"By Crom, Niord," gasped the Cimmerian. "Am I alive, or are we all dead and in Valhalla?"

"We live," grunted the As, busy over Conan's half-frozen feet. "We had to fight our way through an ambush, or we had come up with you before the battle was joined. The corpses were scarce cold when we came upon the field. We did not find you among the dead, so we followed your spoor. In Ymir's name, Conan, why did you wander off into the wastes of the North? We have followed your tracks in the snow for hours. Had a blizzard come up and hidden them, we had never found you, by Ymir!"

"Swear not so often by Ymir," muttered a warrior uneasily, glancing at the distant mountains. "This is his land, and legends say the god bides among yonder peaks."

"I saw a woman," Conan answered hazily. "We met Bragi's men in the plains. I know not how long we fought. I alone lived. I was dizzy and faint. The land lay like a dream before me; only now do all things seem natural and familiar. The woman came and taunted me. She was beautiful as a frozen flame from Hell. A strange madness fell upon me when I looked at her, so I forgot all else in the world. I followed her. Did you not find her tracks? Or the giants in icy mail I slew?"

Niord shook his head. "We found only your tracks in the snow, Conan."

"Then it may be that I am mad," said Conan dazedly. "Yet you yourself are no more real to me than was the golden-locked wench who fled naked across the snows before me. Yet from under my very hands she vanished in icy flame."

"He is delirious," whispered a warrior.

"Not so!" cried an older man, whose eyes were wild and weird. "It was Atali, the daughter of Ymir, the frost giant! To fields of the dead she comes and shows herself to the dying! Myself when a boy I saw her, when I lay half slain on the bloody field of Wolfraven. I saw her walk among the dead in the snows, her naked body gleaming like ivory and her golden hair unbearably bright in the moonlight. I lay and howled like a dying dog because I could not crawl after her. She lures men from stricken fields into the wastelands to be slain by her brothers, the ice giants, who lay men's red hearts smoking on Ymir's board. The Cimmerian has seen Atali, the frost giant's daughter!"

"Bah!" grunted Horsa. "Old Gorm's mind was touched in his youth by a sword cut on the head. Conan was delirious from the fury of the battle; look how his helmet is dinted. Any of those blows might have addled his brain. It was a hallucination he followed into the wastes. He is from the South; what does he know of Atali?"

"You speak truth, perhaps," muttered Conan. "It was all strange and weird—by Crom!"

He broke off, glaring at the object that still dangled from his clenched left fist. The others gaped silently at the veil he held up—a wisp of gossamer that was never spun by human distaff.

The Lair of the Ice Worm

Haunted by Atali's icy beauty and bored with the simple life of the Cimmerian villages, Conan rides south toward the civilized realms, hoping to find a ready market for his sword as a condottiere in the service of various Hyborian princelings. At this time, Conan is about twenty-three.

1.

ALL DAY, the lone rider had breasted the slopes of the Eiglophian Mountains, which strode from east to west across the world like a mighty wall of snow and ice, sundering the northlands of Vanaheim, Asgard, and Hyperborea from the southern kingdoms. In the depth of winter, most of the passes were blocked. With the coming of spring, however, they opened, to afford bands of fierce, light-haired northern barbarians routes by which they could raid the warmer lands to the south.

This rider was alone. At the top of the pass that led southward into the Border Kingdom and Nemedia, he reined in to sit for a moment, looking at the fantastic scene before him.

The sky was a dome of crimson and golden vapors, darkening from the zenith to the eastern horizon with the purple of oncoming evening. But the fiery splendor of the dying day still painted the white crests of the mountains with a deceptively warm-looking rosy radiance. It threw shadows of deep lavender across the frozen surface of a titanic glacier, which wound like an icy serpent from a coomb among the higher peaks, down and down until it curved in front of the pass and then away again to the left, to dwindle in the foothills and turn into a flowing stream of water. He who traveled through the pass had to pick his way cautiously past the margin of the glacier, hoping that he would neither fall into one of its hidden crevasses nor be overwhelmed by an avalanche from the higher slopes. The setting sun turned the glacier into a glittering expanse of crimson and gold. The rocky slopes that rose from the glacier's flanks were dotted with a thin scattering of gnarled, dwarfish trees.

This, the rider knew, was Snow Devil Glacier, also known as the River of Death Ice. He had heard of it, although his years of wandering had never before chanced to take him here. Everything he had heard of this glacier-guarded pass was shadowed by a nameless fear. His own Cimmerian fellow-tribesmen, in their bleak hills to the west, spoke of the Snow Devil in terms of dread, although no one knew why. Often he had wondered at the legends that clustered about the glacier, endowing it with the vague aura of ancient evil. Whole parties had vanished there, men said, never to be heard of again.

The Cimmerian youth named Conan impatiently dismissed these rumors. Doubtless, he thought, the missing men had lacked mountaineering skill and had carelessly strayed out on one of the bridges of thin snow that often masked glacial crevasses. Then the snow bridge had given way, plunging them all to their deaths in the blue-green depths of the glacier. Such things happened often enough, Crom knew; more than one boyhood acquaintance of the young Cimmerian had perished thus. But this was no reason to refer to the Snow Devil with shudders, dark hints, and sidelong glances.

Conan was eager to descend the pass into the low hills

of the Border Kingdom, for he had begun to find the simple life of his native Cimmerian village boring. His ill-fated adventure with a band of golden-haired Æsir on a raid into Vanaheim had brought him hard knocks and no profit. It had also left him with the haunting memory of the icy beauty of Atali, the frost giant's daughter, who had nearly lured him to an icy death.

Altogether, he had had all he wanted of the bleak northlands. He burned to get back to the hot lands of the South, to taste again the joys of silken raiment, golden wine, fine victuals, and soft feminine flesh. Enough, he thought, of the dull round of village life and the Spartan austerities of camp and field!

His horse picked its way to the place where the glacier thrust itself across the direct route to the lowlands. Conan slid off his mount and led the animal along the narrow pathway between the glacier on his left and the lofty, snow-covered slope on his right. His huge bearskin cloak exaggerated even his hulking size. It hid the coat of chain mail and the heavy broadsword at his hip.

His eyes of volcanic blue glowered out from under the brim of a horned helmet, while a scarf was wound around the lower part of his face to protect his lungs from the bite of the cold air of the heights. He carried a slender lance in his free hand. Where the path meandered out over the surface of the glacier, Conan went gingerly, thrusting the point of the lance into the snow where he suspected that it might mask a crevasse. A battle-ax hung by its thong from his saddle.

He neared the end of the narrow path between the glacier and the hillside, where the glacier swung away to the left and the path continued down over a broad, sloping surface, lightly covered with spring snow and broken by boulders and hummocks. Then a scream of terror made him whip around and jerk up his helmeted head.

A bowshot away to his left, where the glacier leveled off before beginning its final descent, a group of shaggy, hulking creatures ringed a slim girl in white furs. Even at this distance, in the clear mountain air, Conan could discern the warm, fresh-cheeked oval of her face and the mane of glossy brown hair that escaped from under her white hood. She was a real beauty.

Without waiting to ponder the matter, Conan threw off his cloak and, using his lance as a pole, vaulted into the saddle. He gathered up the reins and drove his spurs into the horse's ribs. As the startled beast reared a little in the haste with which it bounded forward, Conan opened his mouth to utter the weird and terrible Cimmerian war cry—then shut it again with a snap. As a younger man he would have uttered this shout to hearten himself, but his years of Turanian service had taught him the rudiments of craftiness. There was no use in warning the girl's attackers of his coming any sooner than he must.

They heard his approach soon enough, however. Although the snow muffled his horse's hoofs, the faint jingle of his mail and the creak of his saddle and harness caused one of them to turn. This one shouted and pulled at his neighbor's arm, so that in a few seconds all had turned to see Conan's approach and set themselves to meet it.

There were about a dozen of the mountain men, armed with crude wooden clubs and with stone-headed spears and axes. They were short-limbed, thick-bodied creatures, wrapped in tattered, mangy furs. Small, bloodshot eyes glared out from under beetling brows and sloping foreheads; thick lips drew back to reveal large yellow teeth. They were like leftovers from some earlier stage of human evolution, about which Conan had once heard philosophers argue in the courtyards of Nemedian temples. Just now, however, he was too fully occupied with guiding his horse and aiming his lance to spare such matters more than the barest fleeting thought. Then he crashed among them like a thunderbolt.

2.

Conan knew that the only way to deal with such a number of enemies afoot was to take full advantage of the mobility of the horse—to keep moving, so as never to let them cluster around him. For while his mail would protect his own body from most of their blows, even their crude weapons could quickly bring down his mount. So he drove toward the nearest beast-man, guiding his horse a little to the left.

As the iron lance crushed through bone and hairy flesh, the mountain man screamed, dropped his own weapon, and tried to clutch at the shaft of Conan's spear. The thrust of the horse's motion hurled the sub-man to earth. The lance head went down and the butt rose. As he cantered through the scattered band, Conan dragged his lance free.

Behind him, the mountain men broke into a chorus of yells and screams. They pointed and shouted at one another, issuing a dozen contradictory commands at once. Meanwhile Conan guided his mount in a tight circle and galloped back through the throng. A thrown spear glanced from his mailed shoulder; another opened a small gash in his horse's flank. But he drove his lance into another mountain man and again rode free, leaving behind a wriggling, thrashing body to spatter the snow with scarlet.

At his third charge, the man he speared rolled as he fell, snapping the lance shaft. As he rode clear, Conan threw away the stump of the shaft and seized the haft of the ax that hung from his saddle. As he rode into them once more, he leaned from his saddle. The steel blade flashed fire in the sunset glow as the ax described a huge figure-eight, with one loop to the right and one to the left. On each side, a mountain man fell into the snow with a cloven skull. Crimson drops spattered the snow. A third mountain man, who did not move quickly enough, was knocked down and trampled by Conan's horse.

With a wail of terror, the trampled man staggered to his feet and fled limping. In an instant, the other six had joined him in panic-stricken flight across the glacier. Conan drew rein to watch their shaggy figures dwindle— and then had to leap clear of the saddle as his horse shuddered and fell. A flint-headed spear had been driven deep into the animal's body, just behind Conan's left leg. A glance showed Conan that the beast was dead.

"Crom damn me for a meddling fool!" he growled to himself. Horses were scarce and costly in the northlands. He had ridden this steed all the way from far Zamora. He had stabled and fed and pampered it through the long winter. He had left it behind when he joined the Æsir in their raid, knowing that deep snow and treacherous ice would rob it of most of its usefulness. He had counted upon the faithful beast to get him back to the warm lands, and now it lay dead, all because he had impulsively intervened in a quarrel among the mountain folk that was none of his affair.

As his panting breath slowed and the red mist of battle fury faded out of his eyes, he turned toward the girl for whom he had fought. She stood a few feet away, staring at him wide-eyed.

"Are you all right, lass?" he grunted. "Did the brutes hurt you? Have no fear; I'm not a foe. I am Conan, a Cimmerian."

Her reply came in a dialect he had never heard before. It seemed to be a form of Hyperborean, mixed with words from other tongues—some from Nemedian and others from sources he did not recognize. He found it hard to gather more than half her meaning.

"You fight—like a god," she panted. "I thought—you Ymir come to save Ilga."

As she calmed, he drew the story from her in spurts of words. She was Ilga of the Virunian people, a branch of the Hyperboreans who had strayed into the Border Kingdom. Her folk lived in perpetual war with the hairy cannibals who dwelt in caves among the Eiglophian peaks. The struggle for survival in this barren realm was desperate; she would have been eaten by her captors had not Conan rescued her.

Two days before, she explained, she had set out with a small party of Virunians to cross the pass above Snow Devil Glacier. Thence they planned to journey several days' ride northeast to Sigtona, the nearest of the Hyperborean strongholds. There they had kinsmen, among whom the Virunians hoped to trade at the spring fair. There Ilga's uncle, who accompanied her, also meant to seek a good husband for her. But they had been ambushed by the hairy ones, and only Ilga had survived the terrible battle on the slippery slopes. Her uncle's last command to her, before he fell with his skull cleft by a flint ax, had been to ride like the wind for home.

Before she was out of sight of the mountain men, her horse had fallen on a patch of ice and broken a leg. She had thrown herself clear and, though bruised, had fled afoot. The hairy ones, however, had seen the fall, and a party of them came scampering down over the glacier to seize her. For hours, it seemed, she had run from them. But at last they had caught up with her and ringed her round, as Conan had seen.

Conan grunted his sympathy; his profound dislike of Hyperboreans, based upon his sojourn in a Hyperborean slave pen, did not extend to their women. It was a hard

70

tale, but life in the bleak northlands was grim. He had often heard the like.

Now, however, another problem faced them. Night had fallen, and neither had a horse. The wind was rising, and they would have little chance of surviving through the night on the surface of the glacier. They must find shelter and make a fire, or Snow Devil Glacier would add two more victims to its toll.

3.

Late that night, Conan fell asleep. They had found a hollow beneath an overhang of rock on the side of the glacier, where the ice had melted away enough to let them squeeze in. With their backs to the granite surface of the cliff, deeply scored and striated by the rubbing of the glacier, they had room to stretch out. In front of the hollow rose the flank of the glacier—clear, translucent ice, fissured by cavernous crevasses and tunnels. Although the chill of the ice struck through to their bones, they were still warmer than they would have been on the surface above, where a howling wind was now driving dense clouds of snow before it.

Ilga had been reluctant to accompany Conan, although he made it plain that he meant the lass no harm. She had tugged away from his hand, crying out an unfamiliar word, which sounded something like *yakhmar*. At length, losing patience, he had given her a mild cuff on the side of the head and carried her unconscious to the dank haven of the cave.

Then he had gone out to recover his bearskin cloak and the gear and supplies tied to his saddle. From the rocky slope that rose from the edge of the glacier, he had gathered a double armful of twigs, leaves, and wood, which he had carried to the cave. There, with flint and steel, he had coaxed a small fire into life. It gave more the illusion of warmth than true warmth, for he dared not let it grow too large lest it melt the nearby walls of the glacier and flood them out of their refuge.

The orange gleams of the fire shone deeply into the fissures and tunnels that ran back into the body of the glacier until their windings and branchings were lost in the dim distance. A faint gurgle of running water came to Conan's ears, now and then punctuated by the creak and crack of slowly moving ice.

Conan went out again into the biting wind, to hack from the stiffening body of his horse some thick slabs of meat. These he brought back to the cave to roast on the ends of pointed sticks. The horse steaks, together with slabs of black bread from his saddle bag, washed down with bitter Asgardian beer from a goatskin bottle, made a tough but sustaining repast.

Ilga seemed withdrawn as she ate. At first Conan thought she was still angry with him for the blow. But it was gradually borne upon him that her mind was not on this incident at all. She was, instead, in the grip of stark terror. It was not the normal fear she had felt for the band of shaggy brutes that had pursued her, but a deep, superstitious dread somehow connected with the glacier. When he tried to question her, she could do nothing but whisper the strange word, "*Yakhmar! Yakhmar!*" while her lovely face took on a pale, drawn look of terror. When he tried to get the meaning of the word out of her, she could only make vague gestures, which conveyed nothing to him.

After the meal, warm and weary, they curled up together in his bearskin cloak. Her nearness brought to Conan's mind the thought that a bout of hot love might calm her mind for sleep. His first tentative caresses found her not at all unwilling. Nor was she unresponsive to his youthful ardor; as he soon discovered, she was not new to this game. Before the hour of lovemaking was over.

she was gasping and crying out in her passion. Afterwards, thinking her now relaxed, the Cimmerian rolled over and slept like a dead man.

The girl, however, did not sleep. She lay rigid, staring out at the blackness that yawned in the ice cavities beyond the feeble glow of the banked fire. At last, near dawn, came the thing she dreaded.

It was a faint piping sound—a thin, ullulating thread of music that wound around her mind until it was as helpless as a netted bird. Her heart fluttered against her ribs. She could neither move nor speak, even to rouse the snoring youth beside her.

Then two disks of cold green fire appeared in the mouth of the nearest ice tunnel—two great orbs that burned into her young soul and cast a deathly spell over her. There was no soul or mind behind those flaming disks— only remorseless hunger.

Like one walking in a dream, Ilga rose, letting her side of the bearskin cloak slide to her feet. Naked, a slim white form against the dimness, she went forward into the darkness of the tunnel and vanished. The hellish piping faded and ceased; the cold green eyes wavered and disappeared. And Conan slept on.

4.

Conan awoke suddenly. Some eery premonition—some warning from the barbarian's hyperacute senses—sent its current quivering along the tendrils of his nerves. Like some wary jungle cat, Conan came instantly from deep, dreamless slumber to full wakefulness. He lay without movement, every sense searching the air around him.

Then, with a deep growl rumbling in his mighty chest, the Cimmerian heaved to his feet and found himself alone in the cavern. The girl was gone. But her furs, which

73

she had discarded during their lovemaking, were still there. His brows knotted in a baffled scowl. Danger was still in the air, scrabbling with tenuous fingers at the edges of his nerves.

He hastily donned his garments and weapons. With his ax in his clenched fist, he thrust himself through the narrow space between the overhang and the flank of the glacier. Outside on the snow, the wind had died. Although Conan sensed dawn in the air, no gleam of morning had yet dimmed the diamond blaze of thousands of throbbing stars overhead. A gibbous moon hung low above the western peaks, casting a wan glow of pale gold across the snow fields.

Conan's keen glance raked the snow. He saw no footprints near the overhang, nor any sign of struggle. On the other hand, it was incredible that Ilga should have wandered off into the labyrinth of tunnels and crevasses, where walking was almost impossible even with spiked boots and where a false step could plunge one into one of those cold streams of ice-melt that run along the bottoms of glaciers.

The hairs on Conan's nape prickled at the weirdness of the girl's disappearance. At heart a superstitious barbarian, he feared nothing mortal but was filled with dread and loathing by the uncanny supernatural beings and forces that lurked in the dark corners of his primeval world.

Then, as he continued to search the snow, he went rigid. Something had lately emerged from a gap in the ice a few strides from the overhang. It was huge, long, soft, and sinuous, and it moved without feet. Its writhing track was clearly visible in the curving path that its belly had crushed in the soft whiteness, like some monstrous serpent of the snows.

The setting moon shone faintly, but Conan's wilderness-sharpened eyes easily read the path. This path led, curving around hillocks of snow and outjutting ledges of rock, up the hillside away from the glacier—up, toward the windswept peaks. He doubted that it had gone alone.

As he followed the path, a bulky, black, furry shadow, he passed the place where his dead horse had lain. Now there was little left of the carcass but a few bones. The track of the thing could be discerned about the remains, but only faintly, for the wind had blown loose snow over them.

A little further on, he came upon the girl—or what was left of her. Her head was gone, and with it most of the flesh of her upper body, so that the white bones gleamed like ivory in the dimming moonlight. The protruding bones had been cleaned, as if the flesh had been sucked from them or rasped off by some many-toothed tongue.

Conan was a warrior, the hard song of a hard people, who had seen death in a thousand forms. But now a mighty rage shook him. A few hours before, this slim, warm girl had lain in the mighty circle of his arms, returning passion for passion. Now nothing was left of her but a sprawled, headless thing, like a doll broken and thrown away.

Conan mastered himself to examine the corpse. With a grunt of surprise, he found that it was frozen solid and sheathed in hard ice.

5.

Conan's eyes narrowed thoughtfully. She could not have left his side more than an hour ago, for the cloak had still held some of the warmth from her body when he awoke. In so brief a time, a warm body does not freeze solid, let alone become encased in glittering ice. It was not according to nature.

Then he grunted a coarse expletive. He knew now, with inward loathing and fury, what had borne the sleeping girl from his side. He remembered the half-forgotten legends told around the fire in his Cimmerian boyhood. One of these concerned the dread monster of the snows, the grim Remora—the vampiric ice worm whose name was an almost forgotten whisper of horror in Cimmerian myth.

The higher animals, he knew, radiated heat. Below them in the scale of being came the scaled and plated reptiles and fishes, whose temperature was that of their surroundings. But the Remora, the worm of the ice lands, seemed unique in that it radiated *cold;* at least, that was how Conan would have expressed it. It gave out a sort of bitter cold that could encase a corpse in an armor of ice within minutes. Since none of Conan's fellow-tribesmen claimed to have seen a Remora, Conan had assumed that the creature was long extinct.

This, then, must be the monster that Ilga had dreaded, and of which she had vainly tried to warn him by the name *yakhmar.*

Conan grimly resolved to track the thing to its lair and slay it. His reasons for this decision were vague, even to himself. But, for all his youthful impulsiveness and his wild, lawless nature, he had his own rude code of honor. He liked to keep his word and to fulfill an obligation that he had freely undertaken. While he did not think of himself as a stainless, chivalrous hero, he treated women with a rough kindness that contrasted with the harshness and truculence with which he met those of his own sex. He refrained from forcing his lusts upon women if they were unwilling, and he tried to protect them when he found them dependent upon him.

Now he had failed in his own eyes. In accepting his rough act of love, the girl Ilga had placed herself under his protection. Then, when she needed his strength, he had slumbered unaware like some besotted beast. Not knowing about the hypnotic piping sound by which the Remora paralyzed its victims and by which it had kept

76

him—usually a light sleeper—sound asleep, he cursed himself for a stupid, ignorant fool not to have paid more heed to her warnings. He ground his powerful teeth and bit his lips in rage, determined to wipe out this stain on his code of honor if it cost him his life.

As the sky lightened in the east, Conan returned to the cave. He bundled together his belongings and laid his plans. A few years before, he might have rushed out on the ice worm's trail, trusting to his immense strength and the keen edges of his weapons to see him through. But experience, if it had not yet tamed all his rash impulses, had taught him the beginnings of caution.

It would be impossible to grapple with the ice worm with naked hands. The very touch of the creature meant frozen death. Even his sword and his ax were of doubtful effectiveness. The extreme cold might make their metal brittle, or the cold might run up their hafts and freeze the hand that wielded them.

But—and here a grim smile played over Conan's lips—perhaps he could turn the ice worm's power against itself.

Silently and swiftly he made his preparations. Gorged, the gelid worm would doubtless slumber through the daylight hours. But Conan did not know how long it would take him to reach the creature's lair, and he feared that another gale might wipe out its serpentine track.

6.

As it turned out, it took Conan little more than an hour to find the ice worm's lair. The dawning sun had ascended only a little way above the eastern peaks of the Eiglophians, making the snow fields sparkle like pavements of crushed diamonds, when he stood at last before the mouth of the ice cave into which the writhing snow track led him. This cave opened in the flank of a smaller glacier, a tributary of the Snow Devil. From his elevation,

77

Conan could look back down the slope to where this minor glacier curved to join the main one, like the affluent of a river.

Conan entered the opening. The light of the rising sun glanced and flashed from the translucent ice walls on either side, breaking up into rainbow patterns and polychrome gleams. Conan had the sensation of walking by some magical means through the solid substance of a colossal gem.

Then, as he penetrated deeper into the glacier, the darkness congealed around him. Still, he doggedly set one foot before the other, plodding onward. He raised the collar of his bearskin cloak to protect his face from the numbing cold that poured past him, making his eyeballs ache and forcing him to take short, shallow breaths to keep his lungs from being frosted. Crystals of ice formed like a delicate mask upon his face, to shatter with each movemest and as quickly to re-form. But he went on, carefully holding that which he carried so gingerly inside his cloak.

Then in the gloom before him opened two cold green eyes, which stared into the roots of his soul. These luminous orbs cast a gelid, submarine light of their own. By their faint, fungoid phosphorescence, he could see that there the cavern ended in a round well, which was the ice worm's nest. Coil on undulating coil, its immense length was curled in the hollow of its nest. Its boneless form was covered with the silken nap of thick white fur. Its mouth was merely a jawless, circular opening, now puckered and closed. Above the mouth, the two luminous orbs gleamed out of a smooth, rounded, featureless, eel-like head.

Replete, the ice worm took a few heartbeats to react to Conan's presence. During the countless eons that the thing of the snows had dwelt in the cold silences of Snow Devil Glacier, no puny man-thing had ever challenged it in the frozen depths of its nest. Now its weird, trilling, mind-binding song rose about Conan, pouring over him in lulling, overpowering, narcotic waves.

But it was too late. Conan threw back his cloak to expose his burden. This was his heavy steel horned Asgardian helm, into which he had packed the glowing coals of his fire, and in which the head of his ax also lay buried, held in place by a loop of the chin strap around the handle. A rein from his horse's harness was looped around the ax helve and the chin strap.

Holding the end of the rein in one hand, Conan whirled the whole mass over his head, round and round, as if he were whirling a sling. The rush of air fanned the faintly glowing coals to red, then to yellow, then to white. A stench of burning helmet padding arose.

The ice worm raised its blunt head. Its circular mouth slowly opened, revealing a ring of small, inward-pointing teeth. As the piping sound grew to an intolerable pitch and the black circle of mouth moved toward him, Conan stopped the whirl of the helmet on the end of its thong. He snatched out the ax, whose helve was charred, smoking and flaming where it entered the fiercely glowing ax head. A quick cast sent the incandescent weapon looping into the cavernous maw. Holding the helmet by one of its horns, Conan hurled the glowing coals after the ax. Then he turned and ran.

7.

Conan never quite knew how he reached the exit. The writhing agony from the thing of the snows shook the glacier. Ice cracked thunderously all around him. The draft of interstellar cold no longer wafted out of the tunnel; instead, a blinding, swirling fog of steam choked the air.

Stumbling, slipping, and falling on the slick, uneven

surface of the ice, banging into one side wall of the tunnel and then the other, Conan at last reached the outer air. The glacier trembled beneath his feet with the titanic convulsions of the dying monster within. Plumes of steam wafted from a score of crevasses and caverns on either side of Conan, who, slipping and skidding, ran down the snowy slope. He angled off to one side to get free of the ice. But, before he reached the solid ground of the mountainside, with its jagged boulders and stunted trees, the glacier exploded. When the white-hot steel of the ax head met the frigid interior of the monster, something had to give way.

With a crashing roar, the ice quivered, broke up, hurled glassy fragments into the air, and collapsed into a chaotic mass of ice and pouring water, soon hidden by a vast cloud of vapor. Conan lost his footing, fell, tumbled, rolled, slid, and fetched up with bruising force against a boulder on the edge of the ice flow. Snow stuffed his mouth and blinded his eyes. A big piece of ice up-ended toppled, and struck his boulder, nearly burying him in fragments of ice.

Half stunned, Conan dragged himself out from under the mass of broken ice. Although cautious moving of his limbs showed no bones to be broken, he bore enough bruises to have been in a battle. Above him, a tremendous cloud of vapor and glittering ice crystals whirled upward from the site of the ice worm's cavern, now a black crater. Fragments of ice and slush poured into this crater from all sides. The whole level of the glacier in the area had sunk.

Little by little the scene returned to normal. The biting mountain breeze blew away the clouds of vapor. The water from the melting of the ice froze again. The glacier returned to its usual near-immobility.

Battered and weary, Conan limped down into the pass.

Lamed as he was, he must now walk all the way to far Nemedia or Ophir, unless he could buy, beg, borrow, or steal another horse. But he went with a high heart, turning his bruised face southward—to the golden South, where shining cities lifted tall towers to a balmy sun, and where a strong man with courage and luck could win gold, wine, and soft, full-breasted women.

Queen of the Black Coast

Conan returns to the Hyborian kingdoms, where he serves as a condottiere in Nemedia, Ophir, and finally Argos. In the last-named place, a slight misunderstanding with the law impels him to take the first ship outward bound. He is about twenty-four years old now.

1. Conan Joins the Pirates

Believe green buds awaken in the spring,
   That autumn paints the leaves with somber fire;
Believe I held my heart inviolate
   To lavish on one man my hot desire.
                —THE SONG OF BÊLIT

HOOFS DRUMMED down the street that sloped to the wharfs. The folk that yelled and scattered had only a fleeting glimpse of a mailed figure on a black stallion, a wide scarlet cloak flowing out on the wind. Far up the street came the shout and clatter of pursuit, but the horseman did not look back. He swept out onto the wharfs and jerked the plunging stallion back on its haunches at the very lip of the pier. Seamen gaped up at him, as they stood to the sweep and striped sail of a high-prowed, broad-waisted galley. The master, sturdy and black-bearded, stood in the bows, easing her away from the piles with a boat hook. He yelled angrily as the horseman sprang from the saddle and with a long leap landed squarely on the mid-deck.

"Who invited you aboard?"

"Get under way!" roared the intruder with a fierce gesture that spattered red drops from his broadsword.

"But we're bound for the coasts of Kush!" expostulated the master.

"Then I'm for Kush! Push off, I tell you!" The other cast a quick glance up the street, along which a squad of horsemen were galloping; far behind them toiled a group of archers, crossbows on their shoulders.

"Can you pay for your passage?" demanded the master.

"I pay my way with steel!" roared the man in armor, brandishing the great sword that glittered bluely in the sun. "By Crom, man, if you don't get under way, I'll drench this galley in the blood of its crew!"

The shipmaster was a good judge of men. One glance at the dark, scarred face of the swordsman, hardened with passion, and he shouted a quick order, thrusting strongly against the piles. The galley wallowed out into clear water, the oars began to clack rhythmically; then a puff of wind filled the shimmering sail. The light ship hecled to the gust, then took her course like a swan, gathering headway as she skimmed along.

On the wharfs the riders were shaking their swords, shouting threats and commands that the ship put about, and yelling for the bowmen to hasten before the craft was out of arbalest range.

"Let them rave," grinned the swordsman hardily. "Do you keep her on her course, master steersman."

The master descended from the small deck between the bows, made his way between the rows of oarsmen, and mounted the mid-deck. The stranger stood there with his back to the mast, eyes narrowed alertly, sword ready. The shipman eyed him steadily, careful not to make any move toward the long knife in his belt. He saw a tall, power-fully built figure in a black scale-mail hauberk, burnished greaves, and a blue-steel helmet, from which jutted bull's horns, highly polished. From the mailed shoulders fell the scarlet cloak, blowing in the sea wind. A broad shagreen belt with a golden buckle held the scabbard of the broad-sword he bore. Under the horned helmet, a square-cut black mane contrasted with smoldering blue eyes.

"If we must travel together," said the master, "we may as well be at peace with each other. My name is Tito, li-censed master shipman of the ports of Argos. I am bound for Kush, to trade beads and silks and sugar and brass-hilted swords to the black kings for ivory, copra, copper ore, slaves, and pearls."

The swordsman glanced back at the rapidly receding docks, where the figures still gesticulated helplessly, evi-dently having trouble in finding a boat swift enough to overhaul the fast-sailing galley.

"I am Conan, a Cimmerian," he answered. "I came into Argos seeking employment, but with no wars forward there was nothing to which I might turn my hand."

"Why do the guardsmen pursue you?" asked Tito. "Not that it's any of my business, but I thought perhaps—"

"I've nothing to conceal," replied the Cimmerian. "By Crom, though I've spent considerable time among you civilized peoples, your ways are still beyond my compre-hension.

"Well, last night in a tavern, a captain in the king's guard offered violence to the sweetheart of a young sol-dier, who naturally ran him through. But it seems there is some cursed law against killing guardsmen, and the boy and his girl fled away. It was bruited about that I was seen with them, and so today I was haled into court, and a judge asked me where the lad had gone. I replied that since he was a friend of mine, I could not betray him.

Then the court waxed wroth, and the judge talked a great deal about my duty to the state, and society, and other things I did not understand, and bade me tell where my friend had flown. By this time I was becoming wrathful myself, for I had explained my position.

"But I choked my ire and held my peace, and the judge squalled that I had shown contempt for the court, and that I should be hurled into a dungeon to rot until I betrayed my friend. So then, seeing they were all mad, I drew my sword and cleft the judge's skull; then I cut my way out of the court, and seeing the high constable's stallion tied near by, I rode for the wharfs, where I thought to find a ship bound for foreign parts."

"Well," said Tito hardily, "the courts have fleeced me too often in suits with rich merchants for me to owe them any love. I'll have questions to answer if I ever anchor in that port again, but I can prove I acted under compulsion. You may as well put up your sword. We're peaceable sailors and have nothing against you. Besides, it's as well to have a fighting man like yourself on board. Come up to the poop deck and we'll have a tankard of ale."

"Good enough," readily responded the Cimmerian, sheathing his sword.

The *Argus* was a small, sturdy ship, typical of those trading craft which plied between the ports of Zingara and Argos and the southern coasts, hugging the shoreline and seldom venturing far into the open ocean. It was high of stern, with a tall, curving prow; broad in the waist, sloping beautifully to stem and stern. It was guided by the long sweep from the poop, and propulsion was furnished mainly by the broad striped silk sail, aided by a jibsail. The oars were for use in tacking out of creeks and bays, and during calms. There were ten to the side, five fore and aft of the small mid-deck. The most precious part of the cargo was lashed under this deck and under the fore-deck. The men slept on deck or between the rowers' benches, protected, in bad weather, by canopies. With twenty men at the oars, three at the sweep, and the shipmaster, the crew was complete.

So the *Argus* pushed steadily southward, with consistently fair weather. The sun beat down from day to day with fiercer heat, and the canopies were run up—striped silken cloths that matched the shimmering sail and the shining goldwork on the prow and along the gunwales.

They sighted the coast of Shem—long, rolling meadowlands with the white crowns of the towers of cities in the distance, and horsemen with blue-black beards and hooked noses, who sat their steeds along the shore and eyed the galley with suspicion. She did not put in; there was scant profit in trade with the fierce and wary sons of Shem.

Nor did Master Tito pull into the broad bay where the Styx river emptied its gigantic flood into the ocean, and the massive black castles of Khemi loomed over the blue waters. Ships did not put unasked into this port, where dusky sorcerers wove awful spells in the murk of sacrificial smoke mounting eternally from bloodstained altars where naked women screamed, and where Set, the Old Serpent, arch-demon of the Hyborians but god of the Stygians, was said to writhe his shining coils among his worshippers.

Master Tito gave that dreamy, glass-floored bay a wide berth, even when a serpent-prowed gondola shot from behind a castellated point of land, and naked dusky women, with great red blossoms in their hair, stood and called to his sailors, and posed and postured brazenly.

Now no more shining towers rose inland. They had passed the southern borders of Stygia and were cruising along the coasts of Kush. The sea and the ways of the sea were never-ending mysteries to Conan, whose homeland

86

was among the high hills of the northern uplands. The wanderer was no less of interest to the sturdy seamen, few of whom had ever seen one of his race.

They were characteristic Argossean sailors, short and stockily built. Conan towered above them, and no two of them could match his strength. They were hardy and robust, but his was the endurance and vitality of a wolf, his thews steeled and his nerves whetted by the hardness of his life in the world's wastelands. He was quick to laugh, quick and terrible in his wrath. He was a valiant trencherman, and strong drink was a passion and a weakness with him. Naïve as a child in many ways, unfamiliar with the sophistry of civilization, he was naturally intelligent, jealous of his rights, and dangerous as a hungry tiger. Young in years, he was hardened in warfare and wandering, and his sojourns in many lands were evident in his apparel. His horned helmet was such as was worn by the golden-haired Æsir of Nordheim; his hauberk and greaves were of the finest workmanship of Koth; the fine ring mail which sheathed his arms and legs was of Nemedia; the blade at his girdle was a great Aquilonian broadsword; and his gorgeous scarlet cloak could have been spun nowhere but in Ophir.

So they beat southward, and Master Tito began to look for the high-walled villages of the black people. But they found only smoking ruins on the shore of a bay, littered with naked black bodies. Tito swore.

"I had good trade here, aforetime. This is the work of pirates."

"And if we meet them?" Conan loosened his great blade in its scabbard.

"Mine is no warship. We run, not fight. Yet if it came to a pinch, we have beaten off reavers before, and might do it again; unless it were Bêlit's *Tigress*."

"Who is Bêlit?"

"The wildest she-devil unhanged. Unless I read the signs awrong, it was her butchers who destroyed that village on the bay. May I some day see her dangling from the yardarm! She is called the queen of the Black Coast. She is a Shemite woman, who leads black raiders. They harry the shipping and have sent many a good tradesman to the bottom."

From under the poop deck, Tito brought out quilted jerkins, steel caps, bows, and arrows.

"Little use to resist if we're run down," he grunted. "But it rasps the soul to give up life without a struggle."

It was just at sunrise when the lookout shouted a warning. Around the long point of an island off the starboard bow glided a long lethal shape, a slender, serpentine galley, with a raised deck that ran from stem to stern. Forty oars on each side drove her swiftly through the water, and the low rail swarmed with naked blacks who chanted and clashed spears on oval shields. From the masthead floated a long crimson pennon.

"Bêlit!" yelled Tito, paling. "Yare! Put her about! Into that creek mouth! If we can beach her before they run us down, we have a chance to escape with our lives!"

So, veering sharply, the *Argus* ran for the line of surf that boomed along the palm-fringed shore, Tito striding back and forth, exhorting the panting rowers to greater efforts. The master's black beard bristled, his eyes glared.

"Give me a bow," requested Conan. "It's not my idea of a manly weapon, but I learned archery among the Hyrkanians, and it will go hard if I can't feather a man or so on yonder deck."

Standing on the poop, he watched the serpent-like ship skimming lightly over the waters, and landsman though he was, it was evident to him that the *Argus* would never win that race. Already arrows, arching from the pirate's

88

deck, were falling with a hiss into the sea, not twenty paces astern.

"We'd best stand to it," growled the Cimmerian; "else we'll all die with shafts in our backs, and not a blow dealt."

"Bend to it, dogs!" roared Tito with a passionate gesture of his brawny fist. The bearded rowers grunted, heaving at the oars, while their muscles coiled and knotted, and sweat started out on their hides. The timbers of the stout little galley creaked and groaned as the men fairly ripped her through the water. The wind had fallen; the sail hung limp. Nearer crept the inexorable raiders, and they were still a good mile from the surf when one of the steersmen fell gagging across the sweep, a long arrow through his neck. Tito sprang to take his place, and Conan, bracing his feet wide on the heaving poop deck, lifted his bow. He could see the details of the pirate plainly now. The rowers were protected by a line of raised mantelets along the sides, but the warriors dancing on the narrow deck were in full view. These were painted and plumed, and mostly naked, brandishing spears and spotted shields.

On the raised platform in the bows stood a slim figure whose white skin glistened in dazzling contrast to the glossy ebon hides about it. Bêlit, without a doubt. Conan drew the shaft to his ear—then some whim or qualm stayed his hand and sent the arrow through the body of a tall plumed spearman beside her.

Hand over hand the pirate galley was overhauling the lighter ship. Arrows fell in a rain about the *Argus*, and men cried out. All the steersmen were down, pin-cushioned, and Tito was handling the massive sweep alone, gasping black curses, his braced legs knots of straining thews. Then with a sob he sank down, a long shaft quivering in his sturdy heart. The *Argus* lost headway and rolled

89

in the swell. The men shouted in confusion, and Conan
took command in characteristic fashion.

"Up, lads!" he roared, loosing with a vicious twang of
cord. "Grab your steel and give these dogs a few knocks
before they cut our throats! Useless to bend your backs
any more: they'll board us ere we can row another fifty
paces!"

In desperation the sailors abandoned their oars and
snatched up their weapons. It was valiant, but useless.
They had time for one flight of arrows before the pirate
was upon them. With no one at the sweep, the *Argus*
rolled broadside, and the steel-beaked prow of the raider
crashed into her amidships. Grappling irons crunched into
the side. From the lofty gunwales, the black pirates drove
down a volley of shafts that tore through the quilted
jackets of the doomed sailormen, then sprang down spear
in hand to complete the slaughter. On the deck of the
pirate lay half a dozen bodies, an earnest of Conan's
archery.

The fight on the *Argus* was short and bloody. The stocky
sailors, no match for the tall barbarians, were cut down to
a man. Elsewhere the battle had taken a peculiar turn.
Conan, on the high-pitched poop, was on a level with the
pirate's deck. As the steel prow slashed into the *Argus*,
he braced himself and kept his feet under the shock,
casting away his bow. A tall corsair, bounding over the rail,
was met in midair by the Cimmerian's great sword, which
sheared him cleanly through the torso, so that his body
fell one way and his legs another. Then, with a burst of
fury that left a heap of mangled corpses along the gunwales, Conan was over the rail and on the deck of the
Tigress.

In an instant he was the center of a hurricane of stabbing spears and lashing clubs. But he moved in a blinding
blur of steel. Spears bent on his armor or swished empty

90

air, and his sword sang its death song. The fighting madness of his race was upon him, and with a red mist of unreasoning fury wavering before his blazing eyes, he cleft skulls, smashed breasts, severed limbs, ripped out entrails, and littered the deck like a shambles with a ghastly harvest of brains and blood.

Invulnerable in his armor, his back against the mast, he heaped mangled corpses at his feet until his enemies gave back panting in rage and fear. Then as they lifted their spears to cast them, and he tensed himself to leap and die in the midst of them, a shrill cry froze the lifted arms. They stood like statues, the black giants poised for the spear casts, the mailed swordsman with his dripping blade.

Bêlit sprang before the blacks, beating down their spears. She turned toward Conan, her bosom heaving, her eyes flashing. Fierce fingers of wonder caught at his heart. She was slender, yet formed like a goddess: at once lithe and voluptuous. Her only garment was a broad silken girdle. Her white ivory limbs and the ivory globes of her breasts drove a beat of fierce passion through the Cimmerian's pulse, even in the panting fury of battle. Her rich black hair, black as a Stygian night, fell in rippling burnished clusters down her supple back. Her dark eyes burned on the Cimmerian.

She was untamed as a desert wind, supple and dangerous as a she-panther. She came close to him, heedless of his great blade, dripping with the blood of her warriors. Her supple thigh brushed against it, so close she came to the tall warrior. Her red lips parted as she stared up into his somber menacing eyes.

"Who are you?" she demanded. "By Ishtar, I have never seen your like, though I have ranged the sea from

the coasts of Zingara to the fires of the ultimate South.
Whence come you?"

"From Argos," he answered shortly, alert for treachery.
Let her slim hand move toward her jeweled dagger in her
girdle, and a buffet of his open hand would stretch her
senseless on the deck. Yet in his heart he did not fear; he
had held too many women, civilized or barbarian, in his
iron-thewed arms, not to recognize the light that burned
in the eyes of this one.

"You are no soft Hyborian!" she exclaimed. "You are
fierce and hard as a gray wolf. Those eyes were never
dimmed by city lights; those thews were never softened
by life amid marble walls."

"I am Conan, a Cimmerian," he answered.

To the people of the exotic climes, the North was a
mazy, half-mythical realm, peopled with ferocious blue-
eyed giants who occasionally descended from their icy
fastnesses with torch and sword. Their raids had never
taken them as far south as Shem, and this daughter of
Shem made no distinction among Æsir, Vanir, or Cimmerian. With the unerring instinct of the elemental feminine, she knew she had found her lover, and his race
meant naught, save as it invested him with the glamor
of far lands.

"And I am Bêlit," she cried, as one might say, "I am
queen!"

"Look at me, Conan!" She threw wide her arms. "I am
Bêlit, queen of the Black Coast. O tiger of the North,
you are cold as the snowy mountains which bred you.
Take me and crush me with your fierce love! Go with
me to the ends of the earth and the ends of the sea! I
am a queen by fire and steel and slaughter—be thou my
king!"

His eyes swept the bloodstained ranks, seeking expres-
sions of wrath or jealousy. He saw none. The fury was

gone from the ebon faces. He realized that to these men Bêlit was more than a woman: a goddess whose will was unquestioned. He glanced at the *Argus*, wallowing in the crimson sea-wash, heeling far over, her decks awash, held up by the grappling irons. He glanced at the blue-fringed shore, at the far green hazes of the ocean, at the vibrant figure which stood before him; and his barbaric soul stirred within him. To quest these shining blue realms with that white-skinned young tiger-cat—to love, laugh, wander, and pillage—

"I'll sail with you," he grunted, shaking the red drops from his blade.

"Ho, N'Yaga!" her voice twanged like a bowstring. "Fetch herbs and dress your master's wounds! The rest of you bring aboard the plunder and cast off."

As Conan sat with his back against the poop rail, while the old shaman attended to the cuts on his hands and limbs, the cargo of the ill-fated *Argus* was quickly shifted aboard the *Tigress* and stored in small cabins below deck. Bodies of the crew and of fallen pirates were cast overboard to the swarming sharks, while wounded blacks were laid in the waist to be bandaged. Then the grappling irons were cast off; and, as the *Argus* sank silently into the blood-flecked waters, the *Tigress* moved off southward to the rhythmic clack of the oars.

As they moved out over the glassy blue deep, Bêlit came to the poop. Her eyes were burning like those of a she-panther in the dark as she tore off her ornaments, her sandals, and her silken girdle and cast them at his feet. Rising on tiptoe, arms stretched upward, a quivering line of naked white, she cried to the desperate horde: "Wolves of the blue sea, behold ye now the dance—the mating dance of Bêlit, whose fathers were kings of Asgalun!"

And she danced, like the spin of a desert whirlwind,

like the leaping of a quenchless flame, like the urge of
creation and the urge of death. Her white feet spurned the
bloodstained deck, and dying men forgot death as they
gazed frozen at her. Then, as the white stars glimmered
through the blue velvet dusk, making her whirling body
a blur of ivory fire, with a wild cry she threw herself
at Conan's feet, and the blind flood of the Cimmerian's
desire swept all else away as he crushed her panting form
against the black plates of his corseleted breast.

2. The Black Lotus

In that Dead citadel of crumbling stone
  Her eyes were snared by that unholy sheen,
And curious madness took me by the throat,
  As of a rival lover thrust between.
               —THE SONG OF BÊLIT

The *Tigress* ranged the sea, and the black villages shuddered. Tom-toms beat in the night, with a tale that the
she-devil of the sea had found a mate, an iron man whose
wrath was as that of a wounded lion. And survivors of
butchered Stygian ships named Bêlit with curse, and a
white warrior with fierce blue eyes; so the Stygian princes
remembered this man long and long, and their memory
was a bitter tree, which bore crimson fruit in the years to
come.

But, heedless as a vagrant wind, the *Tigress* cruised the
southern coasts, until she anchored at the mouth of a
broad, sullen river, whose banks were jungle-clouded walls
of mystery.

"This is the river Zarkheba, which is Death," said Bêlit. "Its waters are poisonous. See how dark and murky
they run? Only venomous reptiles live in that river. The
black people shun it. Once a Stygian galley, fleeing from

me, fled up the river and vanished. I anchored in this very spot, and days later, the galley came floating down the dark waters, its decks bloodstained and deserted. Only one man was on board, and he was mad and died gibbering. The cargo was intact, but the crew had vanished into silence and mystery.

"My lover, I believe there is a city somewhere on that river. I have heard tales of giant towers and walls glimpsed afar off by sailors who dared go part way up the river. We fear nothing: Conan, let us go and sack that city!"

Conan agreed. He generally agreed to her plans. Hers was the mind that directed their raids, his the arm that carried out her ideas. It mattered little to him where they sailed or whom they fought, so long as they sailed and fought. He found the life good.

Battle and raid had thinned their crew; only some eighty spearmen remained, scarcely enough to work the long galley. But Bêlit would not take the time to make the long cruise southward to the island kingdoms where she recruited her buccaneers. She was afire with eagerness for her latest venture; so the *Tigress* swung into the river-mouth, the oarsmen pulling strongly as she breasted the broad current.

They rounded the mysterious bend that shut out the sight of the sea, and sunset found them forging steadily against the sluggish flow, avoiding sandbars where strange reptiles coiled. Not even a crocodile did they see, nor any four-legged beast or winged bird coming down to the water's edge to drink. On through the blackness that preceded moonrise they drove, between banks that were solid palisades of darkness, whence came mysterious rustlings and stealthy footfalls, and the gleam of grim eyes. And once an inhuman voice was lifted in awful mockery —the cry of an ape, Bêlit said, adding that the souls of evil men were imprisoned in these manlike animals as punishment for past crimes. But Conan doubted; for once, in a gold-barred cage in an Hyrkanian city, he had seen an abysmal, sad-eyed beast which men told him was an ape, and there had been about it naught of the demoniac malevolence which vibrated in the shrieking laughter that echoed from the black jungle.

Then the moon rose, a splash of blood, ebony-barred, and the jungle awoke in horrific bedlam to greet it. Roars and howls and yells set the black warriors to trembling; but all this noise, Conan noted, came from farther back in the jungle, as if the beasts no less than men shunned the black waters of Zarkheba.

Rising above the black denseness of the trees and above the waving fronds, the moon silvered the river, and their wake became a rippling scintillation of phosphorescent bubbles that widened like a shining road of bursting jewels. The oars dipped into the shining water and came up sheathed in frosty silver. The plumes on the warriors' headpieces nodded in the wind, and the gems on sword hilts and harness sparkled frostily.

The cold light struck icy fire from the jewels in Bêlit's clustered black locks as she stretched her lithe figure on a leopard skin thrown on the deck. Supported on her elbows, her chin resting on her slim hands, she gazed up into the face of Conan, who lounged beside her, his black mane stirring in the faint breeze. Bêlit's eyes were dark jewels burning in the moonlight.

"Mystery and terror are about us, Conan, and we glide into the realm of horror and death," she said. "Are you afraid?"

A shrug of his mailed shoulders was his only answer.

"I am not afraid either," she said meditatively. "I was never afraid. I have looked into the naked fangs of Death too often. Conan, do you fear the gods?"

"I would not tread on their shadow," answered the barbarian conservatively. "Some gods are strong to harm, others, to aid; at least so say their priests. Mitra of the Hyborians must be a strong god, because his people have builded their cities over the world. But even the Hyborians fear Set. And Bel, god of thieves, is a good god. When I was a thief in Zamora I learned of him."

"What of your own gods? I have never heard you call on them."

"Their chief is Crom. He dwells on a great mountain. What use to call on him? Little he cares if men live or die. Better to be silent than to call his attention to you; he will send you dooms, not fortune! He is grim and loveless, but at birth he breathes power to strive and slay into a man's soul. What else shall men ask of the gods?"

"But what of the worlds beyond the river of death?" she persisted.

"There is no hope here or hereafter in the cult of my people," answered Conan. "In this world men struggle and suffer vainly, finding pleasure only in the bright madness of battle; dying, their souls enter a gray, misty realm of clouds and icy winds, to wander cheerlessly throughout eternity."

Bêlit shuddered. "Life, bad as it is, is better than such a destiny. What do you believe, Conan?"

He shrugged his shoulders. "I have known many gods. He who denies them is as blind as he who trusts them too deeply. I seek not beyond death. It may be the blackness averred by the Nemedian skeptics, or Crom's realm of ice and cloud, or the snowy plains and vaulted halls of the Nordheimer's Valhalla. I know not, nor do I care. Let me live deep while I live; let me know the rich juices of red meat and stinging wine on my palate, the hot embrace of white arms, the mad exultation of battle when the blue blades flame and crimson, and I am content. Let teachers and priests and philosophers brood

97

over questions of reality and illusion. I know this: if life is illusion, then I am no less an illusion, and being thus, the illusion is real to me. I live, I burn with life, I love, I slay, and am content."

"But the gods are real," she said, pursuing her own line of thought. "And above all are the gods of the Shemites—Ishtar and Ashtoreth and Derketo and Adonis. Bel, too, is Shemitish, for he was born in ancient Shumir, long, long ago, and went forth laughing, with curled beard and impish wise eyes, to steal the gems of the kings of old times.

"There is life beyond death, I know, and I know this, too, Conan of Cimmeria"—she rose lithely to her knees and caught him in a pantherish embrace—"my love is stronger than any death! I have lain in your arms, panting with the violence of our love; you have held and crushed and conquered me, drawing my soul to your lips with the fierceness of your bruising kisses. My heart is welded to your heart, my soul is part of your soul! Were I still in death and you fighting for life, I would come back from the abyss to aid you—aye, whether my spirit floated from the purple sails on the crystal sea of paradise, or writhed in the molten flames of Hell! I am yours, and all the gods and all their eternities shall not sever us!"

A scream rang from the lookout in the bows. Thrusting Bêlit aside, Conan bounded up, his sword a long silver glitter in the moonlight, his hair bristling at what he saw. The black warrior dangled above the deck, supported by what seemed a dark, pliant tree trunk arching over the rail. Then he realized that it was a gigantic serpent, which had writhed its glistening length up the side of the bow and gripped the luckless warrior in its jaws. Its dripping scales shone leprously in the moonlight as it reared its form high above the deck, while the stricken man screamed

98

and writhed like a mouse in the fangs of a python. Conan rushed into the bows and, swinging his great sword, hewed nearly through the giant truck, which was thicker than a man's body. Blood drenched the rails as the dying monster swayed far out, still gripping its victim, and sank into the river, coil by coil, lashing the water to bloody foam, in which man and reptile vanished together.

Thereafter Conan kept the lookout watch himself, but no other horror came crawling up from the murky depths; and, as dawn whitened over the jungle, he sighted the black fangs of towers jutting up among the trees. He called Bêlit, who slept on the deck, wrapped in his scarlet cloak; and she sprang to his side, eyes blazing. Her lips were parted to call orders to her warriors to take up bows and spears; then her lovely eyes widened.

It was but the ghost of a city on which they looked when they cleared a jutting, jungle-clad point and swung in toward the incurving shore. Weeds and rank river grass grew between the stones of broken piers and shattered paves that had once been streets and spacious plazas and broad courts. From all sides except that toward the river, the jungle crept in, masking fallen columns and crumbling mounds with poisonous green. Here and there buckling towers reeled drunkenly against the morning sky, and broken pillars jutted up among the decaying walls. In the center space, a marble pyramid was spired by a slim column, and on its pinnacle sat or squatted something that Conan supposed to be an image until his keen eyes detected life in it.

"It is a great bird," said one of the warriors, standing in the bows.

"It is a monster bat," insisted another.

"It is an ape," said Bêlit.

Just then the creature spread broad wings and flapped off into the jungle.

"A winged ape," said old N'Yaga uneasily. "Better we had cut our throats than come to this place. It is haunted."

Bêlit mocked at his superstitions and ordered the galley run inshore and tied to the crumbling wharfs. She was the first to spring ashore, closely followed by Conan, and after them trooped the ebon-skinned pirates, white plumes waving in the morning wind, spears ready, eyes rolling dubiously at the surrounding jungle.

Over all brooded a silence as sinister as that of a sleeping serpent. Bêlit posed picturesquely among the ruins, the vibrant life in her lithe figure contrasting strangely with the desolation and decay about her. The sun-flamed up slowly, sullenly, above the jungle, flooding the towers with a dull gold that left shadows lurking beneath the tottering walls. Bêlit pointed to a slim round tower that reeled on its rotting base. A broad expanse of cracked, grass-grown slabs led up to it, flanked by fallen columns, and before it stood a massive altar. Bêlit went swiftly along the ancient floor and stood before it.

"This was the temple of the old ones," she said. "Look —you can see the channels for the blood along the sides of the altar, and the rains of ten thousand years have not washed the dark stains from them. The walls have all fallen away, but this stone block defies time and the elements."

"But who were these old ones?" demanded Conan.

She spread her slim hands helplessly. "Not even in legendry is this city mentioned. But look at the handholes at either end of the altar! Priests often conceal their treasures beneath their altars. Four of you lay hold and see if you can lift it."

She stepped back to make room for them, glancing up at the tower which loomed drunkenly above them. Three of the strongest blacks had gripped the handholds cut into the stone—curiously unsuited to human hands—

when Bêlit sprang back with a sharp cry. They froze in their places, and Conan, bending to aid them, wheeled with a startled curse.

"A snake in the grass," she said, backing away. "Come and slay it; the rest of you bend your backs to the stone."

Conan came quickly toward her, another taking his place. As he impatiently scanned the grass for the reptile, the giant blacks braced their feet, grunted and heaved with their huge muscles coiling and straining under their ebon skin. The altar did not come off the ground, but it revolved suddenly on its side. And simultaneously there was a grinding rumble above and the tower came crashing down, covering the four black men with broken masonry.

A cry of horror rose from their comrades. Bêlit's slim fingers dug into Conan's arm muscles. "There was no serpent," she whispered. "It was but a ruse to call you away. I feared; the old ones guarded their treasure well. Let us clear away the stones."

With herculean labor they did so and lifted out the mangled bodies of the four men. And under them, stained with their blood, the pirates found a crypt carved in the solid stone. The altar, hinged curiously with stone rods and sockets on one side, had served as its lid. And at first glance the crypt seemed brimming with liquid fire, catching the early light with a million blazing facets. Undreamable wealth lay before the eyes of the gaping pirates: diamonds, rubies, bloodstones, sapphires, turquoises, moonstones, opals, emeralds, amethysts, unknown gems that shone like the eyes of evil women. The crypt was filled to the brim with bright stones that the morning sun struck into lambent flame.

With a cry Bêlit dropped to her knees among the bloodstained rubble on the brink and thrust her white arms shoulder-deep into that pool of splendor. She withdrew them, clutching something that brought another cry to her lips—a long string of crimson stones that were like clots of frozen blood strung on a thick gold wire. In their glow the golden sunlight changed to bloody haze.

Bêlit's eyes were like a woman's in a trance. The Shemite soul finds a bright drunkenness in riches and material splendor, and the sight of this treasure might have shaken the soul of a sated emperor of Shushan.

"Take up the jewels, dogs!" her voice was shrill with her emotions.

"Look!" A muscular black arm stabbed toward the *Tigress*, and Bêlit wheeled, her crimson lips asnarl, as if she expected to see a rival corsair sweeping in to despoil her of her plunder. But from the gunwales of the ship a dark shape rose, soaring away over the jungle.

"The devil-ape has been investigating the ship," muttered the blacks uneasily.

"What matter?" cried Bêlit with a curse, raking back a rebellious lock with an impatient hand. "Make a litter of spears and mantles to bear these jewels—where the devil are you going?"

"To look to the galley," grunted Conan. "That bat-thing might have knocked a hole in the bottom, for all we know."

He ran swiftly down the cracked wharf and sprang aboard. A moment's swift examination below decks, and he swore heartily, casting a clouded glance in the direction the bat-being had vanished. He returned hastily to Bêlit, superintending the plundering of the crypt. She had looped the necklace about her neck, and on her naked white bosom the red clots glimmered darkly. A huge naked black stood crotch-deep in the jewel-brimming crypt, scooping up great handfuls of splendor to pass them to the eager hands above. Strings of frozen iridescence

102

hung between his dusky fingers; drops of red fire dripped from his hands, piled high with starlight and rainbow. It was as if a black titan stood straddle-legged in the bright pits of Hell, his lifted hands full of stars.

"That flying devil has staved in the water casks," said Conan. "If we hadn't been so dazed by these stones we'd have heard the noise. We were fools not to have left a man on guard. We can't drink this river water. I'll take twenty men and search for fresh water in the jungle."

She stared at him vaguely, in her eyes the blank blaze of her strange passion, her fingers working at the gems on her breast.

"Very well," she said absently, hardly heeding him. "I'll get the loot aboard."

The jungle closed quickly about them, changing the light from gold to gray. From the arching green branches, creepers dangled like pythons. The warriors fell into single file, creeping through the primordial twilights like black phantoms following a white ghost.

Underbrush was not so thick as Conan had anticipated. The ground was spongy but not slushy. Away from the river, it sloped gradually upward. Deeper and deeper they plunged into the green waving depths, and still there was no sign of water, either running stream or stagnant pool. Conan halted suddenly, his warriors freezing into basaltic statues. In the tense silence that followed, the Cimmerian shook his head irritably.

"Go ahead," he granted to a sub-chief, N'Gora. "March straight on until you can no longer see me; then stop and wait for me. I believe we're being followed. I heard something."

The blacks shuffled their feet uneasily, but did as they were told. As they swung onward, Conan stepped quickly behind a great tree, glaring back along the way they had

103

come. From that leafy fastness anything might emerge. Nothing occurred; the faint sounds of the marching spearmen faded in the distance. Conan suddenly realized that the air was impregnated with an alien and exotic scent. Something gently brushed his temple. He turned quickly. From a cluster of green, curiously leafed stalks, great black blossoms nodded at him. One of these had touched him. They seemed to beckon him, to arch their pliant stems toward him. They spread and rustled, though no wind blew.

He recoiled, recognizing the black lotus, whose juice was death and whose scent brought dream-haunted slumber. But already he felt a subtle lethargy stealing over him. He sought to lift his sword, to hew down the serpentine stalks, but his arm hung lifeless at his side. He opened his mouth to shout to his warriors, but only a faint rattle issued. The next instant, with appalling suddenness, the jungle waved and dimmed out before his eyes; he did not hear the screams that burst out awfully not far away, as his knees collapsed, letting him pitch limply to the earth. Above his prostrate form, the great black blossoms nodded in the windless air.

3. The Horror in the Jungle

Was it a dream the nighted lotus brought?
    Then curst the dream that bought my sluggish life;
And curst each laggard hour that does not see
    Hot blood drip blackly from the crimsoned knife.
                        —THE SONG OF BÊLIT

First there was the blackness of an utter void, with the cold winds of cosmic space blowing through it. Then shapes, vague, monstrous, and evanescent, rolled in dim panorama through the expanse of nothingness, as if the darkness were taking material form. The winds blew and a vortex formed, a whirling pyramid of roaring blackness. From it grew Shape and Dimension; then suddenly, like clouds dispersing, the darkness rolled away on either hand and a huge city of dark green stone rose on the bank of a wide river, flowing through an illimitable plain. Through this city moved beings of alien configuration.

Cast in the mold of humanity, they were distinctly not men. They were winged and of heroic proportions; not a branch on the mysterious stalk of evolution that culminated in man, but the ripe blossom on an alien tree, separate and apart from that stalk. Aside from their wings, in physical appearance they resembled man only as man in his highest form resembles the great apes. In spiritual, esthetic and intellectual development they were superior to man as man is superior to the gorilla. But when they reared their colossal city, man's primal ancestors had not yet risen from the slime of the primordial seas.

These beings were mortal, as are all things built of flesh and blood. They lived, loved, and died, though the individual span of life was enormous. Then, after uncounted millions of years, the Change began. The vista shimmered and wavered, like a picture thrown on a wind-blown curtain. Over the city and the land the ages flowed as waves flow over a beach, and each wave brought alterations. Somewhere on the planet the magnetic centers were shifting; the great glaciers and ice fields were withdrawing toward the new poles.

The littoral of the great river altered. Plains turned into swamps that stank with reptilian life. Where fertile meadows had rolled, forests reared up, growing into dank jungles. The changing ages wrought on the inhabitants of the city as well. They did not migrate to fresher lands. Rea-

105

sons inexplicable to humanity held them to the ancient city and their doom. And as that once rich and mighty land sank deeper and deeper into the black mire of the sunless jungle, so into the chaos of squalling jungle life sank the people of the city. Terrific convulsions shook the earth; the nights were lurid with spouting volcanoes that fringed the dark horizons with red pillars.

After an earthquake that shook down the outer walls and highest towers of the city and caused the river to run black for days with some lethal substance spewed up from the subterranean depths, a frightful chemical change became apparent in the waters the folk had drunk for millenniums uncountable.

Many died who drank of it; and in those who lived, the drinking wrought change, subtle, gradual, and grisly. In adapting themselves to the changing conditions, they had sunk far below their original level. But the lethal waters altered them even more horribly, from generation to more bestial generation. They who had been winged gods became pinioned demons, with all that remained of their ancestors' vast knowledge distorted and perverted and twisted into ghastly paths. As they had risen higher than mankind might dream, so they sank lower than man's maddest nightmares reach. They died fast, by cannibalism, and horrible feuds fought out in the murk of the midnight jungle. And at last among the lichen-grown ruins of their city only a single shape lurked, a stunted, abhorrent perversion of nature.

Then for the first time humans appeared: dark-skinned, hawk-faced men in copper and leather harness, bearing bows—the warriors of prehistoric Stygia. There were only fifty of them, and they were haggard and gaunt with starvation and prolonged effort, stained and scratched with jungle-wandering, with blood-crusted bandages that told

106

of fierce fighting. In their minds was a tale of warfare and defeat, and flight before a stronger tribe which drove them ever southward, until they lost themselves in the green ocean of jungle and river.

Exhausted, they lay down among the ruins where red blossoms that bloom but once in a century waved in the full moon, and sleep fell upon them. And as they slept, a hideous shape crept red-eyed from the shadows and performed weird and awful rites about and above each sleeper. The moon hung in the shadowy sky, painting the jungle red and black; above the sleepers glimmered the crimson blossoms like splashes of blood. Then the moon went down and the eyes of the necromancer were red jewels set in the ebony of night.

When dawn spread its white veil over the river, there were no men to be seen: only a hairy, winged horror that squatted in the center of a ring of fifty great spotted hyenas that pointed quivering muzzles to the ghastly sky and howled like souls in Hell.

Then scene followed scene so swiftly that each tripped over the heels of its predecessor. There was a confusion of movement, a writhing and melting of light and shadows, against a background of black jungle, green stone ruins, and murky river. Black men came up the river in long boats with skulls grinning on the prows, or stole stooping through the trees, spear in hand. They fled screaming through the dark from red eyes and slavering fangs. Howls of dying men shook the shadows; stealthy feet padded through the gloom, vampire eyes blazed redly. There were grisly feasts beneath the moon, across whose red disk a batlike shadow incessantly swept.

Then, abruptly, etched clearly in contrast to these impressionistic glimpses, around the jungled point in the whitening dawn swept a long galley, thronged with shining ebon figures, and in the bows stood a white-skinned giant in blue steel.

It was at this point that Conan first realized that he was dreaming. Until that instant he had had no consciousness of individual existence. But as he saw himself treading the boards of the *Tigress*, he recognized both the existence and the dream, although he did not waken.

Even as he wondered, the scene shifted abruptly to a jungle glade where N'Gora and nineteen black spearmen stood, as if awaiting someone. Even as he realized that it was for he whom they waited, a horror swooped down from the skies and their stolidity was broken by yells of fear. Like men maddened by terror, they threw away their weapons and raced wildly through the jungle, pressed close by the slavering monstrosity that flapped its wings above them.

Chaos and confusion followed this vision, during which Conan feebly struggled to awake. Dimly he seemed to see himself lying under a nodding cluster of black blossoms, while from the bushes a hideous shape crept toward him. With a savage effort he broke the unseen bonds which held him to his dreams, and started upright.

Bewilderment was in the glare he cast about him. Near him swayed the dusky lotus, and he hastened to draw away from it.

In the spongy soil near by there was a track as if an animal had put out a foot, preparatory to emerging from the bushes, then had withdrawn it. It looked like the spoor of an unbelievably large hyena.

He yelled for N'Gora. Primordial silence brooded over the jungle, in which his yells sounded brittle and hollow as mockery. He could not see the sun, but his wilderness-trained instinct told him the day was near its end. A panic rose in him at the thought that he had lain senseless for hours. He hastily followed the tracks of the spearmen, which lay plain in the damp loam before him. They ran in single file, and he soon emerged into a glade—to stop short, the skin crawling between his shoulders as he recognized it as the glade he had seen in his lotus-drugged dream. Shields and spears lay scattered about as if dropped in headlong flight.

And from the tracks which led out of the glade and deeper into the fastnesses, Conan knew that the spearmen had fled, wildly. The footprints overlay one another; they weaved blindly among the trees. And with startling suddenness the hastening Cimmerian came out of the jungle onto a hill-like rock which sloped steeply, to break off abruptly in a sheer precipice forty feet high. And something crouched on the brink.

At first Conan thought it to be a great black gorilla. Then he saw that it was a giant black man that crouched apelike, long arms dangling, froth dripping from the loose lips. It was not until, with a sobbing cry, the creature lifted huge hands and rushed toward him, that Conan recognized N'Gora. The black man gave no heed to Conan's shout as he charged, eyes rolled up to display the whites, teeth gleaming, face an inhuman mask.

With his skin crawling with the horror that madness always instils in the sane, Conan passed his sword through the black man's body; then, avoiding the hooked hands that clawed at him as N'Gora sank down, he strode to the edge of the cliff.

For an instant he stood looking down into the jagged rocks below, where lay N'Gora's spearmen, in limp, distorted attitudes that told of crushed limbs and splintered bones. Not one moved. A cloud of huge black flies buzzed loudly above the blood-splashed stones; the ants had already begun to gnaw at the corpses. On the trees about sat birds of prey, and a jackal, looking up and seeing the man on the cliff, slunk furtively away.

For a little space Conan stood motionless. Then he wheeled and ran back the way he had come, flinging himself with reckless haste through the tall grass and bushes, hurdling creepers that sprawled snakelike across his path. His sword swung low in his right hand, and an unaccustomed pallor tinged his dark face.

The silence that reigned in the jungle was not broken. The sun had set, and great shadows rushed upward from the slime of the black earth. Through the gigantic shades of lurking death and grim desolation, Conan was a speeding glimmer of scarlet and blue steel. No sound in all the solitude was heard except his own quick panting as he burst from the shadows into the dim twilight of the river shore.

He saw the galley shouldering the rotten wharf, the ruins reeling drunkenly in the gray half-light.

And here and there among the stones were spots of raw bright color, as if a careless hand had splashed with a crimson brush.

Again Conan looked on death and destruction. Before him lay his spearmen, nor did they rise to salute him. From the jungle edge to the riverbank, among the rotting pillars and along the broken piers they lay, torn and mangled and half-devoured, chewed travesties of men.

All about the bodies and pieces of bodies were swarms of huge footprints, like those of hyenas.

Conan came silently upon the pier, approaching the galley above whose deck was suspended something that glimmered ivory-white in the faint twilight. Speechless, the Cimmerian looked on the queen of the Black Coast as she hung from the yardarm of her own galley. Between the yard and her throat stretched a line of crimson clots that shone like blood in the gray light.

110

4. The Attack from the Air

The shadows were black around him,
  The dripping jaws gaped wide,
Thicker than rain the red drops fell;
But my love was fiercer than Death's black spell,
Nor all the iron walls of Hell
  Could keep me from his side.
                    —THE SONG OF BÊLIT

The jungle was a black colossus that locked the ruin-littered glade in ebon arms. The moon had not risen; the stars were flecks of hot amber in a breathless sky that reeked of death. On the pyramid among the fallen towers sat Conan the Cimmerian like an iron statue, chin propped on massive fists. Out in the black shadows, stealthy feet padded and red eyes glimmered. The dead lay as they had fallen. But on the deck of the *Tigress*, on a pyre of broken benches, spear shafts, and leopard skins, lay the queen of the Black Coast in her last sleep, wrapped in Conan's scarlet cloak. Like a true queen she lay, with her plunder heaped high about her: silks, cloth-of-gold, silver braid, casks of gems and golden coins, silver ingots, jeweled daggers, and teocallis of gold wedges.

But of the plunder of the accursed city, only the sullen waters of Zarkheba could tell, where Conan had thrown it with a heathen curse. Now he sat grimly on the pyramid, waiting for his unseen foes. The black fury in his soul drove out all fear. What shapes would emerge from the blackness he knew not, nor did he care.

He no longer doubted the visions of the black lotus. He understood that, while waiting for him in the glade, N'Gora and his comrades had been terror-stricken by the winged monster swooping upon them from the sky and, fleeing in blind panic, had fallen over the cliff; all except their chief, who had somehow escaped their fate, though not madness. Meanwhile, or immediately after, or perhaps before, the destruction of those on the riverbank had been accomplished. Conan did not doubt that the slaughter along the river had been massacre rather than battle. Already unmanned by their superstitious fears, the blacks might well have died without striking a blow in their own defense when attacked by their inhuman foes.

Why he had been spared so long, he did not understand, unless the malign entity which ruled the river meant to keep him alive to torture him with grief and fear. All pointed to a human or superhuman intelligence—the breaking of the water casks to divide the forces, the driving of the blacks over the cliff, and last and greatest, the grim jest of the crimson necklace knotted like a hangman's noose about Bêlit's white neck.

Having apparently saved the Cimmerian for the choicest victim and extracted the last ounce of exquisite mental torture, it was likely that the unknown enemy would conclude the drama by sending him after the other victims. No smile bent Conan's grim lips at the thought, but his eyes were lit with iron laughter.

The moon rose, striking fire from the Cimmerian's horned helmet. No call awoke the echoes; yet suddenly the night grew tense and the jungle held its breath. Instinctively Conan loosened the great sword in its sheath. The pyramid on which he rested was four-sided, one—the side toward the jungle—carved in broad steps. In his hand was a Shemite bow, such as Bêlit had taught her pirates to use. A heap of arrows lay at his feet, feathered ends toward him, as he rested on one knee.

Something moved in the blackness under the trees. Etched abruptly in the rising moon, Conan saw a darkly blocked-out head and shoulders, brutish in outline. And now from the shadows dark shapes came silently, swiftly, running low—twenty great spotted hyenas. Their slavering fangs flashed in the moonlight, their eyes blazed as no true beast's eyes ever blazed.

Twenty: then the spears of the pirates had taken toll of the pack, after all. Even as he thought this, Conan drew nock to ear, and at the twang of the string a flame-eyed shadow bounded high and fell writhing. The rest did not falter; on they came, and like a rain of death among them fell the arrows of the Cimmerian, driven with all the force and accuracy of steely thews backed by a hate hot as the slag heaps of Hell.

In his berserk fury he did not miss; the air was filled with feathered destruction. The havoc wrought among the onrushing pack was breath-taking. Less than half of them reached the foot of the pyramid. Others dropped upon the broad steps. Glaring down into the blazing eyes, Conan knew these creatures were not beasts; it was not merely in their unnatural size that he sensed a blasphemous difference. They exuded an aura tangible as the black mist rising from a corpse-littered swamp. By what godless alchemy these beings had been brought into existence, he could not guess; but he knew he faced diabolism blacker than the Well of Skelos.

Springing to his feet, he bent his bow powerfully and drove his last shaft point-blank at a great hairy shape that soared up at his throat. The arrow was a flying beam of moonlight that flashed onward with but a blur in its course, but the were-beast plunged convulsively in midair and crashed headlong, shot through and through.

Then the rest were on him, in a nightmare rush of blazing eyes and dripping fangs. His fiercely driven sword shore the first asunder; then the desperate impact of the others bore him down. He crushed a narrow skull with the pommel of his hilt, feeling the bone splinter and blood and brains gush over his hand; then, dropping the sword, useless at such deadly close quarters, he caught at the throats of the two horrors which were ripping and tearing at him in silent fury. A foul acrid scent almost stifled him, his

113

own sweat blinded him. Only his mail saved him from being ripped to ribbons in an instant. The next, his naked right hand locked on a hairy throat and tore it open. His left hand, missing the throat of the other beast, caught and broke its foreleg. A short yelp, the only cry in that grim battle, and hideously manlike, burst from the maimed beast. At the sick horror of that cry from a bestial throat, Conan involuntarily relaxed his grip.

One, blood gushing from its torn jugular, lunged at him in a last spasm of ferocity and fastened its fangs on his throat—to fall back dead, even as Conan felt the tearing agony of its grip.

The other, springing forward on three legs, was slashing at his belly as a wolf slashes, actually rending the links of his mail. Flinging aside the dying beast, Conan grappled the crippled horror and, with a muscular effort that brought a groan from his blood-flecked lips, he heaved upright, gripping the struggling, tearing fiend in his arms. An instant he reeled off balance, its fetid breath hot on his nostrils, its jaws snapping at his neck; then he hurled it from him, to crash with bone-splintering force down the marble steps.

As he reeled on wide-braced legs, sobbing for breath, the jungle and the moon swimming bloodily to his sight, the thrash of bat wings was loud in his ears. Stooping, he groped for his sword and, swaying upright, braced his feet drunkenly and heaved the great blade above his head with both hands, shaking the blood from his eyes as he sought the air above him for his foe.

Instead of attack from the air, the pyramid staggered suddenly and awfully beneath his feet. He heard a rumbling crackle and saw the tall column above him wave like a wand. Stung to galvanized life, he bounded far out; his feet hit a step, half-way down, which rocked beneath him, and his next desperate leap carried him clear. But even as his heels hit the earth, with a shattering crash like a breaking mountain the pyramid crumpled; the column came

114

thundering down in bursting fragments. For a blind cataclysmic instant the sky seemed to rain shards of marble. Then a rubble of shattered stone lay whitely under the moon.

Conan stirred, throwing off the splinters that half covered him. A glancing blow had knocked off his helmet and momentarily stunned him. Across his legs lay a great piece of the column, pinning him down. He was not sure that his legs were unbroken. His black locks were plastered with sweat; blood trickled from the wounds in his throat and hands. He hitched up on one arm, struggling with the debris that prisoned him.

Then something swept down across the stars and struck the sward near him. Twisting about, he saw it—*the winged one!*

With fearful speed it was rushing upon him, and in that instant Conan had only a confused impression of a gigantic, manlike shape hurtling along on bowed and stunted legs; of huge, hairy arms outstretching misshapen, black-nailed paws; of a malformed head, in whose broad face the only features recognizable as such were a pair of blood-red eyes. It was a thing neither man, beast, nor devil, imbued with characteristics subhuman as well as characteristics superhuman.

But Conan had no time for conscious consecutive thought. He threw himself toward his fallen sword, and his clawing fingers missed it by inches. Desperately he grasped the shard which pinned his legs, and the veins swelled in his temples as he strove to thrust it off him. It gave slowly, but he knew that before he could free himself the monster would be upon him, and he knew that those black-taloned hands were death.

The headlong rush of the winged one had not wavered. It towered over the prostrate Cimmerian like a black shadow, arms thrown wide—a glimmer of white flashed between it and its victim.

In one mad instant she was there—a tense white shape,

115

vibrant with love fierce as a she-panther's. The dazed Cimmerian saw between him and the onrushing death, her lithe figure, shimmering like ivory beneath the moon; he saw the blaze of her dark eyes, the thick cluster of her burnished hair; her bosom heaved, her red lips were parted, she cried out sharp and ringing as the ring of steel as she thrust at the winged monster's breast.

"*Bêlit!*" screamed Conan. She flashed a quick glance toward him, and in her dark eyes he saw her love flaming, a naked elemental thing of raw fire and molten lava. Then she was gone, and the Cimmerian saw only the winged fiend which had staggered back in unwonted fear, arms lifted as if to fend off attack. And he knew that Bêlit in truth lay on her pyre on the *Tigress'* deck. In his ears rang her passionate cry: "Were I still in death and you fighting for life I would come back from the abyss—"

With a terrible cry he heaved upward, hurling the stone aside. The winged one came on again, and Conan sprang to meet it, his veins on fire with madness. The thews started out like cords on his forearms as he swung his great sword, pivoting on his heel with the force of the sweeping arc. Just above the hips it caught the hurtling shape, and the knotted legs fell one way, the torso another as the blade sheared clear through its hairy body.

Conan stood in the moonlit silence, the dripping sword sagging in his hand, staring down at the remnants of his enemy. The red eyes glared up at him with awful life, then glazed and set; the great hands knotted spasmodically and stiffened. And the oldest race in the world was extinct.

Conan lifted his head, mechanically searching for the beast-things that had been its slaves and executioners. None met his gaze. The bodies he saw littering the moon-splashed grass were of men, not beasts: hawk-faced, dark-skinned men, naked, transfixed by arrows or mangled by swordstrokes. And they were crumbling into dust before his eyes.

Why had not the winged master come to the aid of its slaves when he struggled with them? Had it feared to come within reach of fangs that might turn and rend it? Craft and caution had lurked in that misshapen skull, but had not availed in the end.

Turning on his heel, the Cimmerian strode down the rotting wharfs and stepped aboard the galley. A few strokes of his sword cut her adrift, and he went to the sweep-head. The *Tigress* rocked slowly in the sullen water, sliding out sluggishly toward the middle of the river, until the broad current caught her. Conan leaned on the sweep, his somber gaze fixed on the cloak-wrapped shape that lay in state on the pyre the richness of which was equal to the ransom of an empress.

5. The Funeral Pyre

Now we are done with roaming, evermore;
    No more the oars, the windy harp's refrain;
Nor crimson pennon frights the dusky shore;
    Blue girdle of the world, receive again
Her whom thou gavest me.
                                    —THE SONG OF BÊLIT

Again dawn tinged the ocean. A redder glow lit the river mouth. Conan of Cimmeria leaned on his great sword upon the white beach, watching the *Tigress* swinging out on her last voyage. There was no light in his eyes that contemplated the glassy swells. Out of the rolling blue wastes all glory and wonder had gone. A fierce revulsion shook him as he gazed at the green surges that deepened into purple hazes of mystery.

Bêlit had been of the sea; she had lent it splendor and

117

allure. Without her it rolled a barren, dreary, and desolate waste from pole to pole. She belonged to the sea; to its everlasting mystery he returned her. He could do no more. For himself, its glittering blue splendor was more repellent than the leafy fronds which rustled and whispered behind him of vast mysterious wilds beyond them, and into which he must plunge.

No hand was at the sweep of the *Tigress*, no oars drove her through the green water. But a clean tanging wind bellied her silken sail, and as a wild swan cleaves the sky to her nest, she sped seaward, flames mounting higher and higher from her deck to lick at the mast and envelop the figure that lay lapped in scarlet on the shining pyre.

So passed the queen of the Black Coast, and leaning on his red-stained sword, Conan stood silently until the red glow had faded far out in the blue hazes and dawn splashed its rose and gold over the ocean.

The Vale of Lost Women

It is during his partnership with Bêlit that Conan
gains the name Amra, the Lion, which will follow
him all the rest of his career. Bêlit has been the first
great love of his life, and after her death he will
not follow the sea again for several years. Instead,
he plunges inland and joins the first black tribe that
offers him shelter—the warlike Bamulas. In a few
months he has fought and intrigued his way to the
position of war chief of the Bamulas, whose power
grows rapidly under his leadership.

1.

THE THUNDER of the drums and the great elephant-tusk
horns was deafening, but in Livia's ears the clamor seemed
but a confused muttering, dull and far away. As she lay
on the angareb in the great hut, her state bordered between delirium and semi-unconsciousness. Outward sounds
and movements scarcely impinged upon her senses. Her
whole mental vision, though dazed and chaotic, was yet
centered with hideous certitude on the naked, writhing
figure of her brother, blood streaming down his quivering thighs. Against a dim nightmare background of dusky
interweaving shapes and shadows, that white form was
lined in merciless and awful clarity. The air seemed still
to pulsate with an agonized screaming, mingled and inter-
woven obscenely with a rustle of fiendish laughter.

She was not conscious of sensation as an individual, separate and distinct from the rest of the cosmos. She was drowned in a great gulf of pain—was herself but pain crystallized and manifested in flesh. So she lay without conscious thought or motion, while outside the drums bellowed, the horns clamored, and barbaric voices lifted hideous chants, keeping time to naked feet slapping the hard earth and open palms smiting one another softly.

But through her frozen mentality, individual consciousness at last began to seep. A dull wonder that she was still bodily unharmed first made itself manifest. She accepted the miracle without thanksgiving. The matter seemed meaningless. Acting mechanically, she sat up on the angareb and stared dully about her. Her extremities made feeble beginnings of motions, as if responding to blindly awakening nerve centers. Her naked feet scruffed nervously at the hard-beaten dirt floor. Her fingers twitched convulsively at the skirt of the scanty under-tunic which constituted her only garment. Impersonally she remembered that once, it seemed long, long ago, rude hands had torn her other garments from her body, and she had wept with fright and shame. It seemed strange, now, that so small a wrong should have caused her so much woe. The magnitude of outrage and indignity was only relative, after all, like everything else.

The hut door opened, and a woman entered—a lithe, pantherish creature, whose supple body gleamed like polished ebony, adorned only by a wisp of silk twisted about her strutting loins. The whites of her eyeballs reflected the firelight outside, as she rolled them with wicked meaning.

She bore a bamboo dish of food—smoking meat, roasted yams, mealies, unwieldy ingots of native bread —and a vessel of hammered gold, filled with *yarati* beer. These she set down on the angareb, but Livia paid no

120

heed; she sat staring dully at the opposite wall, hung with mats woven of bamboo shoots. The young native woman laughed, with a flash of dark eyes and white teeth; and, with a hiss of spiteful obscenity and a mocking caress that was more gross than her language, she turned and swaggered out of the hut, expressing more taunting insolence with the motions of her hips than any civilized woman could with spoken insults.

Neither the wench's words nor her actions had stirred the surface of Livia's consciousness. All her sensations were still turned inward. Still the vividness of her mental pictures made the visible world seem like an unreal panorama of ghosts and shadows. Mechanically she ate the food and drank the liquor without tasting either.

It was still mechanically that at last she rose and walked unsteadily across the hut, to peer out through a crack between the bamboos. It was an abrupt change in the timbre of the drums and horns that reacted upon some obscure part of her mind and made her seek the cause, without sensible volition.

At first she could make nothing of what she saw; all was chaotic and shadowy, shapes moving and mingling, writhing and twisting, black formless blocks hewed out starkly against a setting of blood-red that dulled and glowed. Then actions and objects assumed their proper proportions, and she made out men and women moving about the fires. The red light glinted on silver and ivory ornaments; white plumes nodded against the glare; naked figures strutted and posed, silhouettes carved out of darkness and limned in crimson.

On an ivory stool, flanked by giants in plumed headpieces and leopard-skin girdles, sat a fat, squat shape, abysmal, repulsive, a toadlike chunk, reeking of the dank rotting jungle and the nighted swamps. The creature's pudgy hands rested on the sleek arch of his belly; his nape was a roll of fat that seemed to thrust his bullethead forward; his eyes, gleaming coals in a dead black stump. Their appalling vitality belied the inert suggestion of the gross body.

As the girl's gaze rested on that figure, her body stiffened and tensed as frantic life surged through her again. From a mindless automaton, she changed suddenly to a sentient mold of live, quivering flesh, stinging and burning. Pain was drowned in hate, so intense it in turn became pain; she felt hard and brittle, as if her body were turning to steel. She felt her hate flow almost tangibly out along the line of her vision; so it seemed to her that the object of her emotion should fall dead from his carven stool because of its force.

But if Bajujh, king of Bakalah, felt any psychic discomfort because of the concentration of his captive, he did not show it. He continued to cram his froglike mouth to capacity with handfuls of mealies scooped up from a vessel held up to him by a kneeling woman, and to stare down a broad lane which was being formed by the action of his subjects in pressing back on either hand.

Down this lane, walled with sweaty black humanity, Livia vaguely realized some important personage would come, judging from the strident clamor of drum and horn. And, as she watched, one came.

A column of fighting men, marching three abreast, advanced toward the ivory stool, a thick line of waving plumes and glinting spears meandering through the motley crowd. At the head of the ebon spearmen strode a figure at the sight of which Livia started violently; her heart seemed to stop, then began to pound again, suffocatingly. Against that dusky background, this man stood out with vivid distinctness. He was clad like his followers in leopard-skin loinclout and plumed headpiece, but he was a white man.

122

It was not in the manner of a supplicant or a subordinate that he strode up to the ivory stool, and sudden silence fell over the throng as he halted before the squatting figure. Livia felt the tenseness, though she only dimly knew what it portended. For a moment Bajujh sat, craning his short neck upward, like a great frog; then, as if pulled against his will by the other's steady glare, he shambled up off his stool, and stood grotesquely bobbing his shaven head.

Instantly the tension was broken. A tremendous shout went up from the massed villagers, and at a gesture from the stranger, his warriors lifted their spears and boomed a salute royale for King Bajujh. Whoever he was, Livia knew the man must indeed be powerful in that wild land, if Bajujh of Bakalah rose to greet him. And power meant military prestige—violence was the only thing respected by those ferocious races.

Thereafter Livia stood with her eyes glued to the crack in the hut wall, watching the stranger. His warriors mingled with the Bakalahs, dancing, feasting, swigging beer. He himself, with a few of his chiefs, sat with Bajujh and the headmen of Bakalah, cross-legged on mats, gorging and guzzling. She saw his hands dipped deep into the cookingpots with the others, saw his muzzle thrust into the beer vessel out of which Bajujh also drank. But she noticed, nevertheless, that he was accorded the respect due a king. Since he had no stool, Bajujh renounced his also, and sat on the mats with his guest. When a new pot of beer was brought, the king of Bakalah barely sipped it before he passed it to the white man. Power! All this ceremonial courtesy pointed to power—strength—prestige! Livia trembled in excitement as a breathless plan began to form in her mind.

So she watched the white man with painful intensity, noting every detail of his appearance. He was tall; neither

123

in height nor in massiveness was he exceeded by many of the giant blacks. He moved with the lithe suppleness of a great panther. When the firelight caught his blue eyes, they burned like blue fire. High-strapped sandals guarded his feet, and from his broad girdle hung a sword in a leather scabbard. His appearance was alien and unfamiliar; Livia had never seen his like, but she made no effort to classify his position among the races of mankind. It was enough that his skin was white.

The hours passed, and gradually the roar of revelry lessened, as men and women sank into drunken sleep. At last Bajujh rose tottering and lifted his hands, less a sign to end the feast than a token of surrender in the contest of gorging and guzzling, and, stumbling, was caught by his warriors, who bore him to his hut. The white man rose, apparently none the worse for the incredible amount of beer he had quaffed, and was escorted to the guest hut by such of the Bakalah headmen as were able to reel along. He disappeared into the hut, and Livia noticed that a dozen of his own spearmen took their places about the structure, spears ready. Evidently the stranger was taking no chances on Bajujh's friendship.

Livia cast her glance about the village, which faintly resembled a dusty Night of Judgment, what with the straggling streets strewn with drunken shapes. She knew that men in full possession of their faculties guarded the outer boma, but the only wakeful men she saw inside the village were the spearmen about the stranger's hut—and some of these were beginning to nod and lean on their spears.

With her heart beating hammer-like, she glided to the back of her prison hut and out the door, passing the snoring guard Bajujh had set over her. Like an ivory shadow she glided across the space between her hut and

124

that occupied by the stranger. On her hands and knees she crawled up to the back of that hut. A black giant squatted here, his plumed head sunk on his knees. She wriggled past him to the wall of the hut. She had first been imprisoned in that hut, and a narrow aperture in the wall, hidden inside by a hanging mat, represented her weak and pathetic attempt at escape. She found the opening, turned sidewise, and wriggled her lithe body through, thrusting the inner mat aside.

Firelight from without faintly illumined the interior of the hut. Even as she thrust back the mat, she heard a muttered curse, felt a viselike grasp in her hair, and was dragged bodily through the aperture and plumped down on her feet.

Staggering with the suddenness of it, she gathered her scattered wits together and raked her disordered tresses out of her eyes, to stare up into the face of the white man who towered over her, amazement written on his dark, scarred face. His sword was naked in his hand, and his eyes blazed like balefire, whether with anger, suspicion or surprise she could not judge. He spoke in a language she could not understand—a tongue which was not a Negro guttural, yet did not have a civilized sound.

"Oh, please!" she begged. "Not so loud. *They* will hear . . ."

"Who are you?" he demanded, speaking Ophirean with a barbarous accent. "By Crom, I never thought to find a white girl in this hellish land!"

"My name is Livia," she answered. "I am Bajujh's captive. Oh, listen, please listen to me! I cannot stay here long. I must return before they miss me from my hut.

"My brother . . ." a sob choked her, then she continued: "My brother was Theteles, and we were of the house of Chelkus, scientists and noblemen of Ophir. By

125

special permission of the king of Stygia, my brother was allowed to go to Kheshatta, the city of magicians, to study their arts, and I accompanied him. He was only a boy—younger than myself . . ." her voice faltered and broke. The stranger said nothing, but stood watching her with burning eyes, his face frowning and unreadable. There was something wild and untamable about him that frightened her and made her nervous and uncertain.

"The black Kushites raided Kheshatta," she continued hurriedly. "We were approaching the city in a camel caravan. Our guards fled, and the raiders carried us away with them. They did us no harm and let us know that they would parley with the Stygians and accept a ransom for our return. But one of the chiefs desired all the ransom for himself, and he and his followers stole us out of the camp one night and fled far to the southeast with us, to the very borders of Kush. There they were attacked and cut down by a band of Bakalah raiders. Theteles and I were dragged into this den of beasts . . ." she sobbed convulsively. ". . . This morning my brother was mutilated and butchered before me . . ." She gagged and went momentarily blind at the memory. "They fed his body to the jackals. How long I lay in a faint I do not know . . ."

Words failing her, she lifted her eyes to the scowling face of the stranger. A mad fury swept over her; she lifted her fists and beat futilely on his mighty breast, which he heeded no more than the buzzing of a fly.

"How can you stand there like a dumb brute?" She screamed in a ghastly whisper. "Are you but a beast like these others? Ah, Mitra, once I thought there was honor in men. Now I know each has his price. You—what do you know of honor—or of mercy or decency? You are a barbarian like the others—only your skin is white; your soul is black as theirs. You care naught that a man of

126

your race has been foully done to death by these dogs—
that I am their slave! Very well."

She fell back from him.

"I will give you a price," she raved, tearing away her
tunic from her ivory breasts. "Am I not fair? Am I not
more desirable than these native wenches? Am I not a
worthy reward for bloodletting? Is not a fair-skinned virgin a price worth slaying for?

"Kill that black dog Bajujh! Let me see his cursed head
roll in the bloody dust! Kill him! *Kill him!*" She beat her
clenched fists together in the agony of her intensity. "Then
take me and do as you wish with me. I will be your
slave!"

He did not speak for an instant but stood like a giant,
brooding figure of slaughter and destruction, fingering his
hilt.

"You speak as if you were free to give yourself at your
pleasure," he said, "as if the gift of your body had power
to swing kingdoms. Why should I kill Bajujh to obtain
you? Women are cheap as plantains in this land, and
their willingness or unwillingness matters as little. You
value yourself too highly. If I wanted you, I wouldn't
have to fight Bajujh to take you. He would rather give
you to me than to fight me."

Livia gasped. All the fire went out of her, the hut
reeled dizzily before her eyes. She staggered and sank in
a crumpled heap on an angareb. Dazed bitterness crushed
her soul as the realization of her utter helplessness was
thrust brutally upon her. The human mind clings un-
consciously to familiar values and ideas, even among surroundings and conditions alien and unrelated to those
environs to which such values and ideas are adapted. In
spite of all Livia had experienced, she had still instinctively supposed a woman's consent the pivotal point of
such a game as she proposed to play. She was stunned by

127

the realization that nothing hinged upon her at all. She could not move men as pawns in a game; she herself was the helpless pawn.

"I see the absurdity of supposing that any man in this corner of the world would act according to rules and customs existent in another corner of the world," she murmured weakly, scarcely conscious of what she was saying, which was indeed only the vocal framing of the thought which overcame her. Stunned by that newest twist of fate, she lay motionless, until the white barbarian's iron fingers closed on her shoulder and lifted her again to her feet.

"You said I was a barbarian," he said harsly, "and that is true, Crom be thanked. If you had had men of the outlands guarding you instead of soft-gutted civilized weaklings, you would not be the slave of a pig this night. I am Conan, a Cimmerian, and I live by the sword's edge. But I am not such a dog as to leave a woman in the clutches of a savage; and though your kind call me a robber, I never forced a woman against her consent. Customs differ in various countries, but if a man is strong enough, he can enforce a few of his native customs anywhere. And no man ever called me a weakling!

"If you were old and ugly as the devil's pet vulture, I'd take you away from Bajujh, simply because of your race. But you are young and beautiful, and I have looked at native sluts until I am sick at the guts. I'll play this game your way, simply because some of your instincts correspond with some of mine. Get back to your hut. Bajujh's too drunk to come to you tonight, and I'll see that he's occupied tomorrow. And tomorrow night it will be Conan's bed you'll warm, not Bajujh's."

"How will it be accomplished?" She was trembling with mingled emotions. "Are these all your warriors?"

"They're enough," he grunted. "Bamulas, every one of

them, and suckled at the teats of war. I came here at Bajujh's request. He wants me to join him in an attack on Jihiji. Tonight we feasted. Tomorrow we hold council. When I get through with him, he'll be holding council in Hell."

"You will break the truce?"

"Truces in this land are made to be broken," he answered grimly. "He would break his truce with Jihiji. And after we'd looted the town together, he'd wipe me out the first time he caught me off guard. What would be blackest treachery in another land, is wisdom here. I have not fought my way alone to the position of war chief of the Bamulas without learning all the lessons the black country teaches. Now go back to your hut and sleep, knowing that it is not for Bajujh but for Conan that you preserve your beauty!"

2.

Through the crack in the bamboo wall, Livia watched, her nerves taut and trembling. All day, since their late waking, bleary and sodden from their debauch of the night before, the people had prepared the feast for the coming night. All day Conan the Cimmerian had sat in the hut of Bajujh, and what had passed between them, Livia could not know. She had fought to hide her excitement from the only person who entered her hut—the vindictive native girl who brought her food and drink. But that ribald wench had been too groggy from her libations of the previous night to notice the change in her captive's demeanor.

Now night had fallen again, fires lighted the village, and once more the chiefs left the king's hut and squatted down in the open space between the huts to feast and hold a final, ceremonious council. This time there was

129

not so much beer-guzzling. Livia noticed the Bamulas casually converging toward the circle where sat the chief men. She saw Bajujh, and sitting opposite him across the eating pots, Conan, laughing and conversing with the giant Aja, Bajujh's war chief.

The Cimmerian was gnawing a great beef bone, and as she watched, she saw him cast a glance across his shoulder. As if it were a signal for which they had been waiting, the Bamulas all turned their gaze toward their chief. Conan rose, still smiling, as if to reach into a nearby cooking pot; then quick as a cat he struck Aja a terrible blow with the heavy bone. The Bakalah war chief slumped over, his skull crushed in, and instantly a frightful yell rent the skies as the Bamulas went into action like blood-mad panthers.

Cooking pots overturned, scalding the squatting women, bamboo walls buckled to the impact of plunging bodies, screams of agony ripped the night, and over all rose the exultant "Yee! yee! yee!" of the maddened Bamulas, the flame of spears that crimsoned in the lurid glow.

Bakalah was a madhouse that reddened into a shambles. The action of the invaders paralyzed the luckless villagers by its unexpected suddenness. No thought of attack by their guests had ever entered their heads. Most of the spears were stacked in the huts, many of the warriors already half drunk. The fall of Aja was a signal that plunged the gleaming blades of the Bamulas into a hundred unsuspecting bodies; after that it was massacre.

At her peephole, Livia stood frozen, white as a statue, her golden locks drawn back and grasped in a knotted cluster with both hands at her temples. Her eyes were dilated, her whole body rigid. The yells of pain and fury smote her tortured nerves like a physical impact; the writhing, slashing forms blurred before her, then sprang out again with horrifying distinctness. She saw spears sink into writhing black bodies, spilling red. She saw clubs swing and descend with brutal force on heads. Brands were kicked out of the fires, scattering sparks; hut thatches smoldered and blazed up. A fresh stridency of anguish cut through the cries, as living victims were hurled head-first into the blazing structures. The scent of scorched flesh began to sicken the air, already rank with reeking sweat and fresh blood.

Livia's overwrought nerves gave way. She cried out again, shrill screams of torment, lost in the roar of flames and slaughter. She beat her temples with her clenched fists. Her reason tottered, changing her cries to more awful peals of hysterical laughter. In vain she sought to keep before her the fact that it was her enemies who were dying thus horribly—that this was as she had madly hoped and plotted—that this ghastly sacrifice was a just repayment for the wrongs done her and hers. Frantic terror held her in its unreasoning grasp.

She was aware of no pity for the victims who were dying wholesale under the dripping spears. Her only emotion was blind, stark, mad, unreasoning fear. She saw Conan, his white form contrasting with the blacks. She saw his sword flash, and men went down around him. Now a struggling knot swept around a fire, and she glimpsed a fat squat shape writhing in its midst. Conan plowed through and was hidden from view by the twisting black figures. From the midst a thin squealing rose unbearably. The press split for an instant, and she had one awful glimpse of a reeling, desperate squat figure, streaming blood. Then the strong crowded in again, and steel flashed in the mob like a beam of lightning through the dusk.

A beastlike baying rose, terrifying in its primitive exultation. Through the mob Conan's tall form pushed its way. He was striding toward the hut where the girl cowered, and in his hand he bore a relic—the firelight gleamed redly on King Bajujh's severed head. The black eyes, glassy now instead of vital, rolled up, revealing only the whites; the jaw hung slack as if in a grin of idiocy; red drops showered thickly along the ground.

Livia gave back with a moaning cry. Conan had paid the price and was coming to claim her, bearing the awful token of his payment. He would grasp her with his bloody fingers, crush her lips with mouth still panting from the slaughter. With the thought came delirium.

With a scream Livia ran across the hut, threw herself against the door in the back wall. It fell open, and she darted across the open space, a flitting white ghost in a realm of black shadows and red flame.

Some obscure instinct led her to the pen where the horses were kept. A warrior was just taking down the bars that separated the horse pen from the main boma, and he yelled in amazement as she darted past him. His hand clutched at her, closed on the neck of her tunic. With a frantic jerk she tore away, leaving the garment in his hand. The horses snorted and stampeded past her, rolling the warrior in the dust—lean, wiry steeds of the Kushite breed, already frantic with the fire and the scent of blood.

Blindly she caught at a flying mane, was jerked off her feet, struck the ground again on her toes, sprang high, pulled and scrambled herself upon the horse's straining back. Mad with fear the herd plunged through the fires, their small hoofs knocking sparks in a blinding shower. The startled black people had a wild glimpse of the girl, clinging naked to the mane of a beast that raced like the wind that streamed out his rider's loose yellow hair. Then straight for the boma the steed bolted, soared breathtakingly into the air, and was gone into the night.

3.

Livia could make no attempt to guide her steed, nor did she feel any need of so doing. The yells and the glow of the fires were fading out behind her; the wind tossed

132

her hair and caressed her naked limbs. She was aware only of a dazed need to hold to the flowing mane and ride, ride, over the rim of the world and away from all agony and grief and horror.

And for hours the wiry steed raced, until, topping a starlit crest, he stumbled and hurled his rider headlong.

She struck on soft cushioning sward, and lay for an instant half stunned, dimly hearing her mount trot away. When she staggered up, the first thing that impressed her was the silence. It was an almost tangible thing—soft, darkly velvet—after the incessant blare of barbaric horns and drums which had maddened her for days. She stared up at the great white stars clustered thickly in the dark sky. There was no moon, yet the starlight illuminated the land, though illusively, with unexpected clusterings of shadow. She stood on a swarded eminence from which the gently molded slopes ran away, soft as velvet under the starlight. Far away in one direction she discerned a dense, dark line of trees which marked the distant forest. Here there was only night and trancelike stillness and a faint breeze blowing through the stars.

The land seemed vast and slumbering. The warm caress of the breeze made her aware of her nakedness, and she wriggled uneasily, spreading her hands over her body. Then she felt the loneliness of the night, and the unbrokenness of the solitude. She was alone; she stood on the summit of land and there was none to see; nothing but night and the whispering wind.

She was suddenly glad of the night and the loneliness. There was none to threaten her, or to seize her with rude, violent hands. She looked before her and saw the slope falling away into a broad valley; there fronds waved thickly and the starlight reflected whitely on many small objects scattered throughout the vale. She thought they were great white blossoms and the thought gave rise to a vague memory; she thought of a valley of which the

133

blacks had spoken with fear: a valley to which had fled the
young women of a strange brown-skinned race which had
inhabited the land before the coming of the ancestors of the
Bakalahs. There, men said, they had turned into white
flowers, had been transformed by the old gods to escape
their ravishers. There no native dared to go.

But into that valley Livia dared to go. She would go down
those grassy slopes which were like velvet under her tender
feet; she would dwell there among the nodding white
blossoms, and no man would ever come to lay rude hands
on her. Conan had said that pacts were made to be broken;
she would break her pact with him. She would go into the
vale of the lost women; she would lose herself in solitude
and stillness . . . even as these dreamy and disjointed
thoughts floated through her consciousness, she was descending the gentle slopes, and the tiers of the valley walls
were rising higher on each hand.

But so gentle were their slopes that when she stood on
the valley floor she did not have the feeling of being imprisoned by rugged walls. All about her floated seas of
shadow, and great white blossoms nodded and whispered
to her. She wandered at random, parting the fronds with
her small hands, listening to the whisper of the wind
through the leaves, finding a childish pleasure in the gurgling of an unseen stream. She moved as in a dream, in
the grasp of a strange unreality. One thought reiterated
itself continually: there she was safe from the brutality of
men. She wept, but the tears were of joy. She lay full-
length upon the sward and clutched the soft grass as if she
would crush her new-found refuge to her breast and hold
it there forever.

She plucked the petals of the blossoms and fashioned
them into a chaplet for her golden hair. Their perfume was
in keeping with all other things in the valley, dreamy,
subtle, enchanting.

So she came at last to a glade in the midst of the valley, and saw there a great stone, hewn as if by human hands, and adorned with ferns and blossoms and chains of flowers. She stood staring at it, and then there was movement and life about her. Turning, she saw figures stealing from the denser shadows—slender brown women, lithe, naked, with blossoms in their night-black hair. Like creatures of a dream they came about her, and they did not speak. But suddenly terror seized her as she looked into their eyes. Those eyes were luminous, radiant in the starshine; but they were not human eyes. The forms were human but in the souls a strange change had been wrought; a change reflected in their glowing eyes. Fear descended on Livia in a wave. The serpent reared its grisly head in her new-found Paradise.

But she could not flee. The lithe brown women were all about her. One, lovelier than the rest, came silently up to the trembling girl, and enfolded her with supple brown arms. Her breath was scented with the same perfume that stole from the white blossoms that waved in the starshine. Her lips pressed Livia's in a long, terrible kiss. The Ophirean felt coldness running through her veins; her limbs turned brittle; like a white statue of marble she lay in the arms of her captress, incapable of speech or movement.

Quick, soft hands lifted her and laid her on the altar-stone amidst a bed of flowers. The brown women joined hands in a ring and moved supplely about the altar, dancing a strange dark measure. Never had the sun or the moon looked on such a dance, and the great white stars grew whiter and glowed with a more luminous light as if its dark witchery struck response in things cosmic and elemental.

And a low chant arose, that was less human than the gurgling of the distant stream; a rustle of voices like the whispering of the blossoms that waved beneath the stars. Livia lay, conscious but without power of movement. It did not occur to her to doubt her sanity. She sought not to reason or analyze; she *was* and these strange beings dancing about her *were*; a dumb realization of existence and recognition of the actuality of nightmare possessed her as she lay helplessly gazing up at the star clustered sky, whence, she somehow knew with more than mortal knowledge, some *thing* would come to her, as it had come long ago to make these naked brown women the soulless beings they now were.

First, high above her, she saw a black dot among the stars, which grew and expanded; it neared her; it swelled to a bat; and still it grew, though its shape did not alter further to any great extent. It hovered over her in the stars, dropping plummet-like earthward, its great wings spread over her; she lay in its shadow. And all about her the chant rose higher, to a soft paean of soulless joy, a welcome to the god which came to claim a fresh sacrifice, fresh and rose-pink as a flower in the dew of dawn.

Now it hung directly over her, and her soul shriveled and grew chill and small at the sight. Its wings were batlike; but its body and the dim face that gazed down upon her were like nothing of sea or earth or air; she knew she looked upon ultimate horror, upon black, cosmic foulness born in night-black gulfs beyond the reach of a madman's wildest dreams.

Breaking the unseen bonds that held her dumb, she screamed awfully. Her cry was answered by a deep, menacing shout. She heard the pounding of rushing feet; all about her there was a swirl as of swift waters; the white blossoms tossed wildly, and the brown women were gone. Over her hovered the great black shadow, and she saw a tall white figure, with plumes nodding in the stars, rushing toward her.

"*Conan!*" The cry broke involuntarily from her lips. With a fierce inarticulate yell, the barbarian sprang into the air, lashing upward with his sword that flamed in the starlight.

The great black wings rose and fell. Livia, dumb with horror, saw the Cimmerian enveloped in the black shadow that hung over him. The man's breath came pantingly; his feet stamped the beaten earth, crushing the white blossoms into the dirt. The rending impact of his blows echoed through the night. He was hurled back and forth like a rat in the grip of a hound; blood splashed thickly on the sward, mingling with the white petals that lay strewn like a carpet.

And then the girl, watching that devilish battle as in a nightmare, saw the black-winged thing waver and stagger in midair; there was a threshing beat of crippled wings, and the monster had torn clear and was soaring upward to mingle and vanish among the stars. Its conqueror staggered dizzily, sword poised, legs wide-braced, staring upward stupidly, amazed at victory but ready to take up again the ghastly battle.

An instant later Conan approached the altar, panting, dripping blood at every step. His massive chest heaved, glistening with perspiration. Blood ran down his arms in streams from his neck and shoulders. As he touched her, the spell on the girl was broken and she scrambled up and slid from the altar, recoiling from his hand. He leaned against the stone, looking down at her, where she cowered at his feet.

"Men saw you ride out of the village," he said. "I followed as soon as I could and picked up your track, though it was no easy task following it by torchlight. I tracked you to the place where your horse threw you, and though the torches were exhausted by then, and I could not find the prints of your bare feet on the sward, I felt sure you

137

had descended into the valley. My men would not follow me, so I came alone on foot. What vale of devils is this? What was that thing?"

"A god," she whispered. "The black people spoke of it —a god from far away and long ago!"

"A devil from the Outer Dark," he grunted. "Oh, they're nothing uncommon. They lurk as thick as fleas outside the belt of light which surrounds this world. I've heard the wise men of Zamora talk of them. Some find their way to earth, but when they do they have to take on some earthly form and flesh of some sort. A man like myself, with a sword, is a match for any amount of fangs and talons, infernal or terrestrial. Come; my men await me beyond the ridge of the valley."

She crouched motionless, unable to find words, while he frowned down at her. Then she spoke: "I ran away from you. I planned to dupe you. I was not going to keep my promise to you; I was yours by the bargain we made, but I would have escaped from you if I could. Punish me as you will."

He shook the sweat and blood from his locks, and sheathed his sword.

"Get up," he grunted. "It was a foul bargain I made. I do not regret that black dog Bajujh, but you are no wench to be bought and sold. The ways of men vary in different lands, but a man need not be a swine wherever he is. After I thought awhile, I saw that to hold you to your bargain would be the same as if I had forced you. Besides, you are not tough enough for this land. You are a child of cities and books and civilized ways—which isn't your fault, but you'd die quickly following the life I thrive on. A dead woman would be no good to me. I will take you to the Stygian borders. The Stygians will send you home to Ophir."

She stared up at him as if she had not heard aright. "Home?" she repeated mechanically. "Home? Ophir? My people? Cities, towers, peace, my *home*?" Suddenly tears welled into her eyes, and sinking to her knees, she embraced his knees in her arms.

"Crom, girl," grunted Conan, embarrassed. "Don't do that. You'd think I was doing you a favor by kicking you out of this country. Haven't I explained that you're not the proper woman for the war chief of the Bamulas?"

The Castle of Terror

*Before he can bring off his plans for building a
black empire with himself at its head, Conan is
thwarted by a succession of natural catastrophes and
the intrigues of his enemies among the Bamulas,
many of whom resent the rise to power in their tribe
of a foreigner. Forced to flee, he heads north through
the equatorial jungle and across the grassy veldt toward the semicivilized kingdom of Kush.*

1. Burning Eyes

BEYOND THE trackless deserts of Stygia lay the vast grasslands of Kush. For over a hundred leagues, there was
naught but endless stretches of thick grass. Here and
there a solitary tree rose to break the gently rolling mon-
otony of the veldt: spiny acacias, sword-leaved dragon
trees, emerald-spired lobelias, and thick-fingered, poisonous spurges. Now and then a rare stream cut a shallow
dell across the prairie, giving rise to a narrow gallery forest along its banks. Herds of zebra, antelope, buffalo, and
other denizens of the savanna drifted athwart the veldt,
grazing as they went.

The grasses whispered and nodded in the wandering
winds beneath skies of deep cobalt in which a fierce tropi-
cal sun blazed blindingly. Now and then clouds boiled
up; a brief thunderstorm roared and blazed with cata-
strophic fury, only to die and clear as quickly as it had
arisen.

Across this limitless waste, as the day died, a lone, silent figure trudged. It was a young giant, strongly built, with gliding thews that swelled under a sun-bronzed hide scored with the white traces of old wounds. Deep of chest and broad of shoulder and long of limb was he; his scanty costume of loinclout and sandals revealed his magnificent physique. His chest, shoulders, and back were burnt nearly as black as the natives of this land.

The tangled locks of an unkempt mane of coarse black hair framed a grim, impassive face. Beneath scowling black brows, fierce eyes of burning blue roamed restlessly from side to side as he marched with a limber, tireless stride across the level lands. His wary gaze pierced the thick, shadowy grasses on either side, reddened by the angry crimson of sunset. Soon night would come swiftly across Kush; under the gloom of its world-shadowing wings, danger and death would prowl the waste.

Yet the lone traveler, Conan of Cimmeria, was not afraid. A barbarian of barbarians, bred on the bleak hills of distant Cimmeria, the iron endurance and fierce vitality of the wild were his, granting him survival where civilized men, though more learned, more courteous, and more sophisticated than he, would miserably have perished. Although the wanderer had gone afoot for eight days, with no food save the game he had slain with the great Bamula hunting bow slung across his back, the mighty barbarian had nowhere nearly approached the limits of his strength.

Long had Conan been accustomed to the Spartan life of the wilderness. Although he had tasted the languid luxuries of civilized life in half the walled, glittering cities of the world, he missed them not. He plodded on toward the distant horizon, now obscured by a murky purple haze.

Behind him lay the dense jungles of the black lands beyond Kush, where fantastic orchids blazed amid foliage

141

of somber dark green, where fierce black tribes hacked a precarious living out of the smothering bush, and where the silence of the dank, shadowed jungle pathways was broken only by the coughing snarl of the hunting leopard, the grunt of the wild pig, the brassy trumpeting of the elephant, or the sudden scream of an angered ape. For over a year, Conan had dwelt there as the war chief of the powerful Bamula tribe. At length the crafty black priests, jealous of his rise to power and resentful of his undisguised contempt for their bloodthirsty gods and their cruel, sanguinary rites, had poisoned the minds of the Bamula warriors against their white-skinned leader.

It had come about in this wise. A time of long, unbroken drought had come upon the tribes of the jungle. With the shrinking of the rivers and the drying up of the water holes had come red, roaring war, as the ebon tribes locked in desperate battle to secure the few remaining sources of the precious fluid. Villages went up in flame; whole clans had been slaughtered and left to rot. Then, in the wake of drought, famine, and war, had come plague to sweep the land.

The malicious tongues of the cunning priests laid these terrors to Conan. It was he, they swore, who had brought these disasters upon Bamula. The gods were angry that a pale-skinned outlander had usurped the ornate stool of a long line of Bamula chieftains. Conan, they persisted, must be flayed and slain with a thousand ingenious torments upon the black altars of the devil-gods of the jungle, or all the people would perish.

Not relishing so grim a fate, Conan had made a swift, devastating reply. A thrust through the body with his great northern broadsword had finished the high priest. Then he had toppled the bloodstained wooden idol of the Bamula deity upon the other shamans and fled into the darkness of the surrounding jungle. He had groped his way for many weary leagues northward, until he reached the region where the crowding forest thinned out and gave way to the open grasslands. Now he meant to cross the savanna on foot to reach the kingdom of Kush, where his barbaric strength and the weight of his sword might find him employment in the service of the dusky monarchs of that ancient land.

Suddenly his thoughts were snatched away from contemplation of the past by a thrill of danger. Some primal instinct of survival alerted him to the presence of peril. He halted and stared about him through the long shadows cast by the setting sun. As the hairs of his nape bristled with the touch of unseen menace, the giant barbarian searched the air with sensitive nostrils and probed the gloom with smoldering eyes. Although he could neither see nor smell anything, the mysterious sense of danger of the wilderness-bred told him that peril was near. He felt the feathery touch of invisible eyes and whirled to glimpse a pair of large orbs, glowing in the gloom.

Almost in the same instant, the blazing eyes vanished. So short had been his glimpse and so utter the disappearance that he was tempted to shrug off the sight as a product of his imagination. He turned and went forward again, but now he was on the alert. As he continued his journey, flaming eyes opened again amid the thick shadows of dense grasses, to follow his silent progress. Tawny, sinuous forms glided after him on soundless feet. The lions of Kush were on his track, lusting for hot blood and fresh flesh.

2. The Circle of Death

An hour later, night had fallen over the savanna, save for a narrow band of sunset glow along the western horizon, against which an occasional small, gnarled tree of the veldt stood up in black silhouette. And Conan had almost reached the limits of his endurance. Thrice lionesses had rushed upon him out of the shadows to right or to left. Thrice he had driven them off with the flying death of his arrows. Although it was hard to shoot straight in the gathering dark, an explosive snarl from the charging cats had thrice told him of hits, although he had no way of knowing whether he had slain or only wounded the deadly predators.

But now his quiver was empty, and he knew it was only a matter of time before the silent marauders pulled him down. There were eight or ten lions on his track now, and even the grim barbarian felt a pang of despair. Even if his mighty sword accounted for one or two of the attackers, the rest would tear him into gory pieces before he could slash or thrust again. Conan had encountered lions before and knew their enormous strength, which enabled them to pick up and drag a whole zebra as easily as a cat does a mouse. Although Conan was one of the strongest men of his time, once a lion got its claws and teeth into him that strength would be no more effective than that of a small child.

Conan ran on. He had been running now for the better part of an hour, with a long, loping stride that ate up the leagues. At first he had run effortlessly, but now the grueling exertions of his flight through the black jungles and his eight-day trek across the plain began to take their toll. His eyes blurred; the muscles of his legs ached. Every beat of his bursting heart seemed to drain away the strength remaining in his giant form.

He prayed to his savage gods for the moon to emerge from the dense, stormy clouds that veiled most of the sky. He prayed for a hillock or a tree to break the gently rolling flatness of the plain, or even a boulder against which he could set his back to make a last stand against the pride.

But the gods heard not. The only trees in this region were dwarfish, thorny growths, which rose to a height of six or eight feet and then spread their branches out horizontally in a mushroom shape. If he managed to climb such a tree despite the thorns, it would be easy for the first lion to reach the base to spring upon him from below and bear him to the ground in one leap. The only hillocks were termite nests, some rising several feet in height but too small for purposes of defense. There was nothing to do but run on.

To lighten himself, he had cast aside the great hunting bow when he had spent his last shaft, although it wrenched his heart to throw away the splendid weapon. Quiver and straps soon followed. He was now stripped to a mere loinclout of leopard hide, the high-laced sandals that clad his feet, his goatskin water bag, and the heavy broadsword, which he now carried scabbarded in one fist. To part with these would mean surrendering his last hope.

The lions were now almost at his heels. He could smell the strong reek of their lithe bodies and hear their panting breath. Any moment, now, they would close in upon him, and he would be making his last furious fight for life before they pulled him down.

He expected his pursuers to follow their age-old tactics. The oldest male—the chief of the pride—would follow directly behind him, with the younger males on either flank. The swifter lionesses would range ahead on either side in a crescent formation until they were far enough ahead of him to close the circle and trap him. Then they would all rush in upon him at once, making any effective defense impossible.

Suddenly, the land was flooded with light. The round, silver eye of the rising moon glared down upon the broad plains, bathing the racing figure of the giant barbarian with her gaze and drawing lines of pale silver fire along the rippling sinews of the lions as they loped at his heels, washing their short, silken fur with her ghostly radiance.

Conan's wary eye caught the moonfire on rippling fur ahead to his left, and he knew that the encirclement was nearly complete. As he braced himself to meet the charge, however, he was astounded to see the same lioness veer off and halt. In two strides he was past her. As he went, he saw that the young lioness on his right had also stopped short. She squatted motionless on the grass with tail twitching and lashing. A curious sound, half roar and half wail, came from her fanged jaws.

Conan dared to slow his run and glance back. To his utter astonishment, he saw that the entire pride had halted as if at some invisible barrier. They stood in a snarling line with fangs gleaming like silver in the moonlight. Earth-shaking roars of baffled rage came from their throats.

Conan's eyes narrowed thoughtfully, and his scowling brows knotted in puzzlement. What had halted the pride at the very moment when they had made sure of their prey? What unseen force had annulled the fury of the chase? He stood for a moment facing them, sword in hand, wondering if they would resume their charge. But the lions stayed where they were, growling and roaring from foam-dripping jaws.

Then Conan observed a curious thing. The place where the lions had halted seemed to mark a line of demarcation across the plain. On the further side grew thick, long, lush grasses. At the invisible boundary, however, the grass became thin, stubbly, and ill-nourished, with broad patches of bare earth. Although Conan could not clearly distinguish colors by moonlight alone, it seemed to him that the grasses on the hither side of the line lacked the normal green color of growing things. Instead, the grasses around his feet seemed dry and gray, as if leached of all vitality.

To either side, in the bright moonlight, he could see the region of dead grasses curve away into the distance, as if he stood alone in a vast circle of death.

3. The Black Citadel

Although he still ached with weariness, the brief pause had given Conan the strength to continue his progress. Since he did not know the nature of the invisible line that had halted the lions, he could not tell how long this mysterious influence would continue to hold them at bay. Therefore he preferred to put as much distance between the pride and himself as possible.

Soon he saw a dark mass take form out of the dimness ahead of him. He went forward even more warily than before, sword in hand and eyes searching the hazy immensities of this domain. The moonlight was still brilliant, but its radiance became obscure with distance as if veiled by some thickening haze. So, at first, Conan could make nothing of the black, featureless mass that lifted out of the plain before him, save for its size and its stillness. Like some colossal idol of primitive devil worship, hewn from a mountain of black stone by some unknown beings in time's dawn, the dark mass squatted motionless amid the dead gray grass.

As Conan came nearer, details emerged from the dark, featureless blur. He saw that it was a tremendous edifice, which lay partly in ruins on the plains of Kush—a colossal structure erected by unknown hands for some nameless purpose. It looked like a castle or fortress of some sort, but of an architectural type that Conan had never seen. Made of dense black stone, it rose in a complex façade of pillars and terraces and battlements, whose alignment seemed oddly awry. It baffled the view. The eye followed mind-twisting curves that seemed subtly wrong, weirdly distorted. The huge structure gave the impression of a chaotic lack of order, as if its builders had not been quite sane.

Conan wrenched his gaze from the vertiginous curves of this misshapen mass of masonry, merely to look upon which made him dizzy. He thought he could at last perceive why the beasts of the veldt avoided this crumbling pile. It somehow exuded an aura of menace and horror. Perhaps, during the millennia that the black citadel had squatted on the plains, the animals had come to dread it and to avoid its shadowy precincts, until such habits of avoidance were now instinctive.

The moon dimmed suddenly as high-piled storm clouds again darkened her ageless face. Distant thunder grumbled, and Conan's searching gaze caught the sulfurous flicker of lightning among the boiling masses of cloud. One of those quick, tempestuous thunderstorms of the savanna was about to break.

Conan hesitated. On the one hand, curiosity and a desire for shelter from the coming storm drew him to the crumbled stronghold. On the other, his barbarian's mind held a deep-rooted aversion to the supernatural. Toward earthly, mortal dangers he was fearless to the point of rashness, but otherworldly perils could send the tendrils of panic quivering along his nerves. And something about this mysterious structure hinted at the supernatural. He could feel its menace in the deepest layers of his consciousness.

A louder rumble of thunder decided him. Taking an iron grip on his nerves, he strode confidently into the dark portal, naked steel in hand, and vanished within.

4. *The Serpent Men*

Conan prowled the length of the high-vaulted hall, finding nothing that lived. Dust and dead leaves littered the black pave. Moldering rubbish was heaped in the corners and around the bases of towering stone columns. However old this pile of masonry was, evidently no living thing had dwelt therein for centuries.

The hall, revealed by another brief appearance of the moon, was two stories high. A balustrated balcony ran around the second floor. Curious to probe deeper into the mystery of this enigmatic structure which squatted here on the plain many leagues from any other stone building, Conan roamed the corridors, which wound as sinuously as a serpent's track. He poked into dusty chambers whose original purpose he could not even guess.

The castle was of staggering size, even to one who had seen the temple of the spider-god at Yezud in Zamora and the palace of King Yildiz at Aghrapur in Turan. A good part of it—one whole wing, in fact—had fallen into a featureless mass of tumbled black blocks, but the part that remained more or less intact was still the largest building that Conan had seen. Its antiquity was beyond guessing. The black onyx of which it was wrought was unlike any stone that Conan had seen in this part of the world. It must have been brought across immense distances why, Conan could not imagine.

Some features of the bizarre architecture of the structure reminded Conan of ancient tombs in accursed Zamora. Others suggested forbidden temples that he had glimpsed in far Hyrkania during his mercenary service with the Turanians. But whether the black castle had been erected primarily as a tomb, a fortress, a palace, or a temple, or some combination of these, he could not tell.

Then, too, there was a disturbing alienage about the castle that made him obscurely uneasy. Even as the façades seemed to have been built according to the canons of some alien geometry, so the interior contained baffling features. The steps of the stairways, for example, were much broader and shallower than was required for human feet. The doorways were too tall and too narrow, so that Conan had to turn sideways to get through them.

The walls were sculptured in low relief with coiling, geometrical arabesques of baffling, hypnotic complexity. Conan found that he had to wrench his gaze away from the sculptured walls by force of will, lest his mind be entrapped and held by the cryptic symbols formed by the writhing lines.

In fact, everything about this strange, baffling enigma in stone reminded Conan of serpents—the winding corridors, the writhing decoration, and even, he thought, a faint trace of a musky, ophidian odor.

Conan halted, brows knotted. Could this unknown ruin have been raised by the serpent folk of ancient Valusia? The day of that pre-human people lay an unthinkable interval in the past, before the dawn of man himself, in the dim mists of time when giant reptiles ruled the earth. Or ever the Seven Empires arose in the days before the Cataclysm—even before Atlantis arose from the depths of the Western Ocean—the serpent people had reigned. They had vanished long before the coming of man—but not entirely.

Around the campfires in the bleak hills of Cimmeria and again in the marbled courts of the temples of Nemedia, Conan had heard the legend of Kull, the Atlantean king of Valusia. The snake people had survived here and there by means of their magic, which enabled them to appear to others as ordinary human beings. But Kull had stumbled upon their secret and had purged his realm clean of their taint, wiping them out with fire and sword.

Still, might not the black castle, with its alien architecture, be a relic of that remote era, when men contended for the rule of the planet with these reptilian survivors of lost ages?

5. *Whispering Shadows*

The first thunderstorm missed the black castle. There was a brief patter of raindrops on the crumbling stonework and a trickle of water through holes in the roof. Then the lightning and thunder diminished as the storm passed off to westward, leaving the moon to shine unobstructed once more through the gaps in the stone. But other storms followed, muttering and flickering out of the east.

Conan slept uneasily in a corner of the balcony above the great hall, tossing and turning like some wary animal that dimly senses the approach of danger. Caution had made him suspicious of sleeping in the hall before the wide-open doors. Even though the circle of death seemed to bar the denizens of the plains, he did not trust the unseen force that held the beasts at bay.

A dozen times he started awake, clutching at his sword and probing the soft shadows with his eyes, searching for whatever had aroused him. A dozen times he found nothing in the gloomy vastness of the ancient wreck. Each time he composed himself for slumber again, however, dim shadows clustered around him, and he half-heard whispering voices.

Growling a weary curse to his barbaric gods, the Cimmerian damned all shadows and echoes to the eleven scarlet Hells of his mythology and threw himself down again, striving to slumber. At length he fell into a deep sleep. And in that sleep there came upon him a strange dream.

It seemed that, although his body slept, his spirit waked and was watchful. To the immaterial eyes of his *ka*, as the Stygians called it, the gloomy balcony was filled with a dim glow of blood-hued light from some unseen source. This was neither the silvery sheen of the moon, which cast slanting beams into the hall through gaps in the

151

stone, nor the pallid flicker of distant lightning. By this sanguine radiance, Conan's spirit could see drifting shadows, which flitted like cloudy bats among the black marble columns—shadows with glaring eyes filled with mindless hunger—shadows that whispered in an all but inaudible cacophony of mocking laughter and bestial cries.

Conan's spirit somehow knew that these whispering shadows were the ghosts of thousands of sentient beings, who had died within this ancient structure. How he knew this, he could not say, but to his *ka* it was a plain fact. The unknown people who had raised this enormous ruin —whether the serpent men of Valusian legend or some other forgotten race—had drenched the marble altars of the black castle with the blood of thousands. The ghosts of their victims were chained forever to this castle of terror. Perhaps they were held earthbound by some powerful spell of prehuman sorcery. Perhaps it was the same spell that kept out the beasts of the veldt.

But this was not all. The ghosts of the black castle hungered for the blood of the living—for the blood of Conan.

His exhausted body lay chained in ensorcelled slumber while shadowy phantoms flitted about him, tearing at him with impalpable fingers. But a spirit cannot harm a living being unless it first manifests itself on the physical plane and assumes material form. These gibbering shadow hordes were weak. Not for years had a man defied the ancient curse to set foot within the black castle, enabling them to feed. Enfeebled by long starvation, they could no longer easily materialize into a shambling horde of ghoul-things.

Somehow, the spirit of the dreaming Conan knew this. While his body slept on, his *ka* observed movements on the astral plane and watched the vampiric shadows as they beat insubstantial wings about his sleeping head and slashed with impalpable claws at his pulsing throat. But for all their voiceless frenzy, they could harm him not. Bound by the spell, he slept on.

After an indefinite time, a change took place in the ruddy luminance of the astral plane. The specters were clustering together into a shapeless mass of thickening shadows. Mindless dead things though they were, hunger drove them into an uncanny alliance. Each ghost possessed a small store of that vital energy that went toward bodily materialization. Now each phantom mingled its slim supply of energy with that of its shadowy brethren.

Gradually, a terrible shape, fed by the life force of ten thousand ghosts, began to materialize. In the dim gloom of the black marble balcony, it slowly formed out of a swirling cloud of shadowy particles.

And Conan slept on.

6. *The Hundred Heads*

Thunder crashed deafeningly; lightning blazed with sulfurous fires above the darkened plain, whence the moonlight had fled again. The thick-piled storm clouds burst, soaking the grassy swales with a torrential downpour.

The Stygian slave raiders had ridden all night, pressing southward toward the forests beyond Kush. Their expedition had thus far been fruitless; not one black of the nomadic hunting and herding tribes of the savanna had fallen into their hands. Whether war or pestilence had swept the land bare of humankind, or whether the tribesmen, warned of the coming of the slavers, had fled beyond reach, they did not know.

In any case, it seemed that they would do better among the lush jungles of the South. The forest Negroes dwelt in permanent villages, which the slavers could surround and take by surprise with a quick dawn rush, catching the inhabitants like fish in a net. Villagers too old, too young, or too sickly to endure the trek back to Stygia they would slay out of hand. Then they would drive the remaining wretches, fettered together to form a human chain, northward.

There were forty Stygians, well-mounted warriors in helms and chain-mail hauberks. They were tall, swarthy, hawk-faced men, powerfully muscled. They were hardened marauders—tough, shrewd, fearless, and merciless, with no more compunction about killing a non-Stygian than most men have about slapping a gnat.

Now the first downpour of the storm swept their column. Winds whipped their woolen cloaks and linen robes and blew their horses' manes into their faces. The almost continuous blaze of lightning dazzled them.

Their leader sighted the black castle, looming above the grasslands, for the blazing lightning made it visible in the rain-veiled dark. He shouted a guttural command and drove his spurs into the ribs of his big black mare. The others spurred after him and rode up to the frowning bastions with a clatter of hoofs, a creaking of leather, and a jingle of mail. In the blur of rain and night, the abnormality of the façade was not visible, and the Stygians were eager to get under shelter before they were soaked.

They came stamping in, cursing and bellowing and shaking the water from their cloaks. In a trice, the gloomy silence of the ruin was broken with a clamor of noise. Brushwood and dead leaves were gathered; flint and steel were struck. Soon a smoking, sputtering fire leaped up in the midst of the cracked marble floor, to paint the sculptured walls with rich orange.

The men flung down their saddlebags, stripped off wet burnooses, and spread them to dry. They struggled out of their coats of mail and set to rubbing the moisture from them with oily rags. They opened their saddlebags and sank strong white teeth into round loaves of hard, stale bread.

Outside, the storm bellowed and flashed. Streams of rainwater, like little waterfalls, poured through gaps in the masonry. But the Stygians heeded them not.

On the balcony above, Conan stood silently, awake but trembling with shudders that wracked his powerful body. With the cloudburst, the spell that held him captive had broken. Starting up, he glared about for the shadowy conclave of ghosts that he had seen form in his dream. When the lightning flashed, he thought he glimpsed a dark, amorphous form at the far end of the balcony, but he did not care to go closer to investigate.

While he pondered the problem of how to quit the balcony without coming in reach of the Thing, the Stygians came stamping and roaring in. They were hardly an improvement on the ghosts. Given half a chance, they would be delighted to capture him for their slave gang. For all his immense strength and skill at arms, Conan knew that no man can fight forty well-armed foes at once. Unless he instantly cut his way out and escaped, they would bring him down. He faced either a swift death or a bitter life of groaning drudgery in a Stygian slave pen. He was not sure which he preferred.

If the Stygians distracted Conan's attention from the phantoms, they likewise distracted the attention of the phantoms from Conan. In their mindless hunger, the shadow-things ignored the Cimmerian in favor of the forty Stygians encamped below. Here was living flesh and vital force enough to glut their phantasmal lusts thrice over. Like autumn leaves, they drifted over the balustrade and down from the balcony into the hall below.

The Stygians sprawled around their fire, passing a bottle of wine from hand to hand and talking in their guttural tongue. Although Conan knew only a few words of Stygian, from the intonations and gestures he could follow the course of the argument. The leader—a clean-shaven giant, as tall as the Cimmerian—swore that he would not venture into the downpour on such a night. They would await the dawn in this crumbling ruin. At least, the roof seemed to be still sound in places, and a man could lie here out of the drip.

When several more bottles had been emptied, the Stygians, now warm and dry, composed themselves for sleep. The fire burned low, for the brushwood with which they fed it could not long sustain a strong blaze. The leader pointed to one of his men and spoke a harsh sentence. The man protested, but after some argument he heaved himself up with a groan and pulled on his coat of mail. He, Conan realized, had been chosen to stand the first watch.

Presently, with sword in hand and shield on arm, the sentry was standing in the shadows at the margin of the light of the dying fire. From time to time he walked slowly up and down the length of the hall, pausing to peer into the winding corridors or out through the front doors, where the storm was in retreat.

While the sentry stood in the main doorway with his back to his comrades, a grim shape formed among the snoring band of slavers. It grew slowly out of wavering clouds of insubstantial shadows. The compound creature that gradually took shape was made up of the vital force of thousands of dead beings. It became a ghastly form— a huge bulk that sprouted countless malformed limbs and appendages. A dozen squat legs supported its monstrous weight. From its top, like grisly fruit, sprouted scores of heads: some lifelike, with shaggy hair and brows; others mere lumps in which eyes, ears, mouths, and nostrils were arranged at random.

156

The sight of the hundred-headed monster in that dimly firelit hall was enough to freeze the blood of the stoutest with terror. Conan felt his nape hairs rise and his skin crawl with revulsion as he stared down upon the scene.

The thing lurched across the floor. Leaning unsteadily down, it clutched one of the Stygians with half a dozen grasping claws. As the man awoke with a scream, the nightmare Thing tore its victim apart, spattering his sleeping comrades with gory, dripping fragments of the man.

7. Flight from Nightmare

In an instant, the Stygians were on their feet. Hardbitten ravagers though they were, the sight was frightful enough to wring yells of terror from some. Wheeling at the first scream, the sentry rushed back into the hall to hack at the monster with his sword. Bellowing commands, the leader snatched up the nearest weapon and fell to. The rest, although unarmored, disheveled, and confused, seized sword and spear to defend themselves against the shape that shambled and slew among them.

Swords hacked into misshapen thighs; spears plunged into the swollen, swaying belly. Clutching hands and arms were hacked away to thud, jerking and grasping, to the floor. But, seeming to feel no pain, the monster snatched up man after man. Some Stygians had their heads twisted off by strangling hands. Others were seized by the feet and battered to gory remnants against the pillars.

As the Cimmerian watched from above, a dozen Stygians were battered or torn to death. The ghastly wounds inflicted on the monster by the weapons of the Stygians instantly closed up and healed. Severed heads and arms were replaced by new members, which sprouted from the bulbous body.

Seeing that the Stygians had no chance against the

monster, Conan resolved to take his leave while the Thing
was still occupied with the slavers and before it turned
its attention to him. Thinking it unwise to enter the hall,
he sought a more direct exit. He climbed out through a
window. This let on to a roof terrace of broken tiles,
where a false step could drop him through a gap in the
pavement to ground level.

The rain had slackened to a drizzle. The moon, now
nearly overhead, showed intermittent beams again. Looking down from the parapet that bounded the terrace,
Conan found a place where the exterior carvings, together
with climbing vines, provided means of descent. With the
lithe grace of an ape, he lowered himself hand over hand
down the weirdly carven façade.

Now the moon glazed out in full glory, lighting the
courtyard below where the Stygians' horses stood teth-
ered, moving and whinnying uneasily at the sounds of
mortal combat that came from the great hall. Over the
roar of battle sounded screams of agony as man after man
was torn limb from limb.

Conan dropped, landing lightly on the earth of the
courtyard. He sprinted for the great black mare that had
belonged to the leader of the slavers. He would have
liked to linger to loot the bodies, for he needed their
armor and other supplies. The mail shirt he had worn
as Bêlit's piratical partner had long since succumbed to
wear and rust, and his flight from Bamula had been too
hasty to allow him to equip himself more completely.
But no force on earth could have drawn him into that
hall, where a horror of living death still stalked and slew.

As the young Cimmerian untethered the horse he had
chosen, a screaming figure burst from the entrance and
came pelting across the courtyard toward him. Conan
saw that it was the man who had stood the first sentry-
go. The Stygian's helmet and mail shirt had protected him

just enough to enable him to survive the massacre of his comrades.

Conan opened his mouth to speak. There was no love lost between him and the Stygian people; nevertheless, if this Stygian were the only survivor of his party, Conan would have been willing to form a rogues' alliance with him, however temporary, until they could reach more settled country.

But Conan had no chance to make such a proposal, for the experience had driven the burly Stygian mad. His eyes blazed wildly in the moonlight, and foam dripped from his lips. He rushed straight upon Conan, whirling a scimitar so that the moonlight flashed upon it and shrieking, "Back to your hell, O demon!"

The primitive survival instinct of the wilderness-bred Cimmerian flashed into action without conscious thought. By the time the man was within striking distance, Conan's own sword had cleared its scabbard. Again and gain, steel clanged against steel, striking sparks. As the wild-eyed Stygian swung back for another slash, Conan drove his point into the madman's throat. The Stygian gurgled, swayed, and toppled.

For an instant, Conan leaned on the mare's saddle bow, panting. The duel had been short but fierce, and the Stygian had been no mean antagonist.

From within the ancient pile of stone, no more cries of terror rang. There was naught but an ominous silence. Then Conan heard slow, heavy, shuffling footsteps. Had the ogreish thing slaughtered them all? Was it dragging its misshapen bulk toward the door, to emerge into the courtyard?

Conan did not wait to find out. With trembling fingers he unlaced the dead man's hauberk and pulled the mail shirt off. He also collected the Stygian's helmet and shield, the latter made from the hide of one of the great, thick-skinned beasts of the veldt. He hastily tied these trophies to the saddle, vaulted upon the steed, wrenched at the reins, and kicked the mare's ribs. He galloped out of the ruined courtyard into the region of withered grass. With every stride of the flying hoofs, the castle of ancient evil fell behind.

Somewhere beyond the circle of dead grass, perhaps the hungry lions still prowled. But Conan did not care. After the ghostly horrors of the black citadel, he would gladly take his chances with mere lions.

The Snout in the Dark

*Continuing his northward trek, now speeded by
his possession of a horse, Conan at last reaches the
semicivilized kingdom of Kush. This is the land to
which the name "Kush" properly applies, although
Conan, like other northerners, tends to use the term
loosely to mean any of the Negro countries south
of the deserts of Stygia. Here an opportunity to display his prowess at arms soon presents itself.*

1. The Thing in the Dark

AMBOOLA OF Kush awakened slowly, his senses still sluggish from the wine he had guzzled at the feast the night
before. For a muddled moment, he could not remember
where he was. The moonlight, streaming through the
small barred window, high up on one wall, shone on unfamiliar surroundings. Then he remembered that he was
lying in the upper cell of the prison into which Queen
Tananda had thrown him.

There had, he suspected, been a drug in his wine. While
he sprawled helplessly, barely conscious, two black giants
of the queen's guard had laid hands upon him and upon
the Lord Aahmes, the queen's cousin, and hustled them
away to their cells. The last thing he remembered was a
brief statement from the queen, like the crack of a whip:
"So you villains would plot to overthrow me, would you?
You shall see what befalls traitors!"

As the giant black warrior moved, a clank of metal

made him aware of fetters on his wrists and ankles, connected by chains to massive iron staples set in the wall. He strained his eyes to pierce the fetid gloom around him. At least, he thought, he still lived. Even Tananda had to think twice about slaying the commander of the Black Spearmen—the backbone of the army of Kush and the hero of the lower castes of the kingdom.

What most puzzled Amboola was the charge of conspiracy with Aahmes. To be sure, he and the princeling had been good friends. They had hunted and guzzled and gambled together, and Aahmes had complained privately to Amboola about the queen, whose cruel heart was as cunning and treacherous as her dusky body was desirable. But things had never gotten to the point of actual conspiracy. Aahmes was not the man for that sort of thing anyway—a good-natured, easygoing young fellow with no interest in politics or power. Some informer, seeking to advance his own prospects at the cost of others, must have laid false accusations before the queen.

Amboola examined his fetters. For all his strength, he knew he could not break them, nor yet the chains that held them. Neither could he hope to pull the staples loose from the wall. He knew, because he had overseen their installation himself.

He knew what the next step would be. The queen would have him and Aahmes tortured, to wring from them the details of their conspiracy and the names of their fellow plotters. For all his barbaric courage, Amboola quailed at the prospect. Perhaps his best hope would lie in accusing all the lords and grandees of Kush of complicity. Tananda could not punish them all. If she tried to, the imaginary conspiracy she feared would quickly become a fact . . .

Suddenly, Amboola was cold sober. An icy sensation scuttled up his spine. Something—a living, breathing presence—was in the room with him.

With a low cry, he started up and stared about him, straining his eyes to pierce the darkness that clung about him like the shadowy wings of death. By the faint light that came through the small barred window, the officer could just make out a terrible and grisly shape. An icy hand clutched at his heart, which through a score of battles had never, until this hour, known fear.

A shapeless gray fog hovered in the gloom. Seething mists swirled like a nest of coiling serpents, as the phantom form congealed into solidity. Stark terror lay on Amboola's writhing lips and shone in his rolling eyes as he saw the thing that condensed slowly into being out of empty air.

First he saw a piglike snout, covered with coarse bristles, which thrust into the shaft of dim luminescence that came through the window. Then he began to make out a hulking form amidst the shadows—something huge, misshapen, and bestial, which nevertheless stood upright. To a piglike head was now added thick, hairy arms ending in rudimentary hands, like those of a baboon.

With a piercing shriek, Amboola sprang up—and then the motionless thing moved, with the paralyzing speed of a monster in a nightmare. The black warrior had one frenzied glimpse of champing, foaming jaws, of great chisel-like tusks, of small, piggish eyes that blazed with red fury through the dark. Then the brutish paws clamped his flesh in a viselike grip; tusks tore and slashed . . .

Presently the moonlight fell upon a black shape, sprawled on the floor in a widening pool of blood. The grayish, shambling thing that a moment before had been savaging the black warrior was gone, dissolved into the impalpable mist from which it had taken form.

2. *The Invisible Terror*

"Tuthmes!" The voice was urgent—as urgent as the fist that hammered on the teakwood door of the house of the most ambitious nobleman of Kush. "Lord Tuth-mes! Let me in! The devil is loose again!"

The door opened, and Tuthmes stood within the portal —a tall, slender, aristocratic figure, with the narrow features and dusky skin of his caste. He was wrapped in robes of white silk as if for bed and held a small bronze lamp in his hand.

"What is it, Afari?" he asked.

The visitor, the whites of his eyes flashing, burst into the room. He panted as if from a long run. He was a lean, wiry, dark-skinned man in a white jubbah, shorter than Tuthmes and with his Negroid ancestry more prominent in his features. For all his haste, he took care to close the door before he answered.

"Amboola! He is dead! In the Red Tower!"

"What?" exclaimed Tuthmes. "Tananda dared to execute the commander of the Black Spears?"

"No, no, no! She would not be such a fool, surely. He was not executed but murdered. Something got into his cell—how, Set only knows—and tore his throat out, stamped in his ribs, and smashed his skull. By Derketa's snaky locks, I have seen many dead men, but never one less lovely in death than Amboola. Tuthmes, it is the work of the demon, of whom the black people murmur! The invisible terror is again loose in Meroê!" Afari clutched the small paste idol of his protector god, which hung from a thong around his scrawny neck. "Amboola's throat was bitten out, and the marks of the teeth were not like those of a lion or an ape. It was as if they had been made by razor-sharp chisels!"

"When was this done?"

"Some time about midnight. Guards in the lower part of the tower, watching the stair that leads up to the cell in which he was imprisoned, heard him cry out. They rushed up the stairs, burst into the cell, and found him

164

lying as I have said. I was sleeping in the lower part of the tower, as you bade me. Having seen, I came straight here, bidding the guards to say naught to anyone."

Tuthmes smiled a cool, impassive smile that was not pleasant to see. He murmured: "You know Tananda's mad rages. Having thrown Amboola and her cousin Aahmes into prison, she might well have had Amboola slain and the corpse maltreated to look like the work of the monster that has long haunted the land. Might she not, now?"

Comprehension dawned in the eyes of the minister. Tuthmes, taking Afari's arm, continued: "Go, now, and strike before the queen can learn of it. First, take a detachment of black spearmen to the Red Tower and slay the guards for sleeping at their duty. Be sure you let it be known that you do it by my orders. That will show the blacks that I have avenged their commander and remove a weapon from Tananda's hand. Kill them before she can have it done.

"Then spread word to the other chief nobles. If this be Tananda's way of dealing with the powerful ones of her realm, we had all best be on the alert.

"Then go into the Outer City and find old Ageera, the witch-smeller. Do not tell him flatly that Tananda caused this deed to be done, but hint at it."

Afari shuddered. "How can a common man lie to that devil? His eyes are like coals of fire; they seem to look into depths unnamable. I have seen him make corpses rise and walk, and skulls champ and grind their fleshless jaws."

"Don't lie," answered Tuthmes. "Simply hint to him of your own suspicions. After all, even if a demon *did* slay Amboola, some human being summoned it out of the night. Perhaps Tananda is behind this, after all. So go quickly!"

When Afari, mulling intensely over his patron's commands, had departed, Tuthmes stood for a moment in the midst of his chamber, which was hung with tapestries of barbaric magnificence. Blue smoke seeped through a domed censer of pierced brass in one corner. Tuthmes called: "Muru!"

Bare feet scuffed the floor. An arras of dull crimson cloth, hung athwart one wall, was thrust back, and an immensely tall, thin man ducked his head under the lintel of the hidden door and entered the room.

"I am here, master," he said.

The man, who towered over even the tall Tuthmes, wore a large piece of scarlet cloth, hung like a toga from one shoulder. Although his skin was as black as jet, his features were narrow and aquiline, like those of the ruling caste of Meroê. The woolly hair of his head was trimmed into a fantastic, crested shape.

"Is *it* back in its cell?" inquired Tuthmes.

"It is."

"Is all secure?"

"Aye, my lord."

Tuthmes frowned. "How can you be sure that it will always obey your commands and then return to you? How know you that some day, when you release it, it will not slay you and flee back to whatever unholy dimension it calls home?"

Muru spread his hands. "The spells I learned from my master, the exiled Stygian wizard, to control the demon, have never failed."

Tuthmes gave the sorcerer a piercing look. "Meseems you wizards spend most of your lives in exile. How do I know that some enemy will not bribe you to turn the monster loose on me some day?"

"Oh, master, think not such thoughts! Without your protection, whither should I go? The Kushites despise me, for I am not of their race; and for reasons you know, I cannot return to Kordafa."

"Hm. Well, take good care of your demon, for we may have more use for it soon. That loose-tongued fool, Afari, loves nothing more than to appear wise in the opinions of others. He will spread the tale of Amboola's murder, embellished with my hints of the queen's rôle, to a hundred waiting ears. The breach between Tananda and her lords will widen, and I shall reap the benefit."

Chuckling with rare good humor, Tuthmes splashed wine into two silver cups and handed one to the gaunt sorcerer, who accepted it with a silent bow. Tuthmes continued:

"Of course, he will not mention that he began the whole charade with his false accusations against Amboola and Aahmes—without orders from me, too. He knows not that—thanks to your necromantic skill, friend Muru —I know all about this. He pretends to be devoted to my cause and faction but would sell us out in an instant if he thought he could gain thereby. His ultimate ambition is to wed Tananda and rule Kush as royal consort. When I am king, I shall need a more trustworthy tool than Afari."

Sipping the wine, Tuthmes mused: "Ever since the late king, her brother, perished in battle with the Stygians, Tananda has clung insecurely to the ivory throne, playing one faction off against another. But she lacks the character to hold power in a land whose tradition does not accept the rule of a woman. She is a rash, impulsive wanton, whose only method of securing power is to slay whatever noble she most fears at the moment, thus alerting and antagonizing the rest.

"Be sure to keep a close watch on Afari, O Muru. And keep your demon on a tight rein. We shall need the creature again."

When the Kordafan had left, ducking his head once more to get through the doorway, Tuthmes mounted a staircase of polished mahogany. He came out upon the flat, moonlit roof of his palace.

Looking over the parapet, he saw below him the silent streets of the Inner City of Meroê. He saw the palaces, the gardens, and the great inner square into which, at an instant's notice, a thousand black horsemen could ride from the courts of the adjoining barracks.

Looking farther, he saw the great bronze gates of the Inner City and, beyond them, the Outer City. Meroê stood in the midst of a great plain of rolling grasslands, which stretched—broken only by occasional low hills—to the horizon. A narrow river, meandering across the grasslands, touched the straggling edges of the Outer City.

A lofty, massive wall, which enclosed the palaces of the ruling caste, separated the Inner and Outer Cities. The rulers were descendants of Stygians who, centuries ago, had come southward to hack out an empire and mix their proud blood with that of their black subjects. The Inner City was well laid out, with regular streets and squares, buildings of stone, and gardens.

The Outer City, on the other hand, was a sprawling wilderness of mud huts. Its streets straggled into irregular open spaces. The black people of Kush, the aboriginal inhabitants of the country, dwelt in the Outer City. None but the ruling caste lived in the Inner City, except for their servants and the black horsemen who served as their guardsmen.

Tuthmes glanced out over that vast expanse of huts. Fires glowed in the ragged squares; torches swayed to and fro in the wandering streets. From time to time he caught a snatch of song, a barbaric chant that thrummed with an undertone of wrath or blood lust. Tuthmes drew his cloak more closely about him and shivered.

Advancing across the roof, he halted at the sight of a

figure sleeping under a palm in the artificial garden. When stirred by Tuthmes' toe, this man awoke and sprang up.

"There is no need for speech," cautioned Tuthmes. "The deed is done. Amboola is dead; and, before dawn, all Meroê will know he was murdered by Tananda."

"And the—the devil?" whispered the man, shivering.

"Safely back in its cell. Harken, Shubba; it is time you were gone. Search among the Shemites until you find a suitable woman—a white woman. Bring her speedily here. If you return within the moon, I will give you her weight in silver. If you fail, I will hang your head from that palm tree."

Shubba prostrated himself and touched his forehead to the dust. Then, rising, he hurried from the roof. Tuthmes glanced again toward the Outer City. The fires seemed somehow to glow more fiercely, and a drum had begun to emit an ominous monotone. A sudden clamor of furious yells welled up to the stars.

"They have heard that Amboola is dead," muttered Tuthmes, and again a strong shudder shook his frame.

3. Tananda Rides

Dawn lit the skies above Meroê with crimson flame. Shafts of rich, ruddy light struck through the misty air and glanced from the copper-sheathed domes and spires of the stone-walled Inner City. Soon the people of Meroê were astir. In the Outer City, statuesque black women walked to the market square with gourds and baskets on their heads, while young girls chattered and laughed on their way to the wells. Naked children fought and played in the dust or chased each other through the narrow streets. Giant black men squatted in the doorways of their thatched huts, working at their trades, or lolled on the ground in the shade.

In the market square, merchants squatted under striped

169

awnings, displaying pots and other manufactures, and vegetables and other produce, on the littered pavement. Black folks chaffered and bargained with endless talk over plaintains, banana beer, and hammered brass ornaments. Smiths crouched over little charcoal fires, laboriously beating out iron hoes, knives, and spearheads. The hot sun blazed down on all—the sweat, mirth, anger, nakedness, strength, squalor, and vigor of the black people of Kush.

Suddenly there came a change in the pattern, a new note in the timbre. With a clatter of hoofs, a group of horsemen rode by in the direction of the great gate of the Inner City. There were half a dozen men and a woman, who dominated the group.

Her skin was a dusky brown; her hair, a thick, black mass, caught back and confined by a golden fillet. Besides the sandals on her feet and the jewel-crusted golden plates that partly covered her full breasts, her only garment was a short silken skirt girdled at the waist. Her features were straight; her bold, scintillant eyes, full of challenge and sureness. She handled the slim Kushite horse with ease and certitude by means of a jeweled bridle and palm-wide, gilt-worked reins of scarlet leather. Her sandaled feet stood in wide silver stirrups, and a gazelle lay across her saddle bow. A pair of slender coursing hounds trotted close behind her horse.

As the woman rode by, work and chatter ceased. The black faces grew sullen; the murky eyes burned redly. The blacks turned their heads to whisper in one another's ears, and the whispers grew to an audible, sinister murmur.

The youth who rode at the woman's stirrup became nervous. He glanced ahead, along the winding street. Estimating the distance to the bronze gates, not yet in view between the huts, he whispered, "The people grow ugly,

Highness. It was folly to ride through the Outer City today."

"All the black dogs in Kush shall not keep me from my hunting!" replied the woman. "If any threaten, ride them down."

"Easier said than done," muttered the youth, scanning the silent throng. "They are coming from their houses and massing thick along the street—look there!"

They entered a wide, ragged square, where the black folk swarmed. On one side of this square stood a house of dried mud and palm trunks, larger than its neighbors, with a cluster of skulls above the doorway. This was the temple of Jullah, which the ruling caste contemptuously called the devil-devil house. The black folk worshiped Jullah in opposition to Set, the serpent-god of their rulers and of their Stygian ancestors.

The black folk thronged in this square, sullenly staring at the horsemen. There was an air of menace in their attitude. Tananda, for the first time feeling a slight nervousness, failed to notice another rider, approaching the square along another street. This rider would ordinarily have attracted attention, for he was neither brown nor black. He was a white man, a powerful figure in chain mail and helmet.

"These dogs mean mischief," muttered the youth at Tananda's side, half drawing his curved sword. The other guardsmen—black men like the folk around them—drew closer about her but did not draw their blades. The low, sullen muttering grew louder, although no movement was made.

"Push through them," ordered Tananda, spurring her horse. The blacks gave back sullenly before her advance.

Then, suddenly, from the devil-devil house came a lean, black figure. It was old Ageera, the witch-smeller, clad only in a loincloth. Pointing at Tananda, he yelled: "There

171

she rides, she whose hands are dipped in blood! She who murdered Amboola!"

His shout was the spark that set off the explosion. A vast roar arose from the mob. They surged forward, screaming, "Death to Tananda!"

In an instant, a hundred black hands were clawing at the legs of the riders. The youth reined between Tananda and the mob, but a flying stone shattered his skull. The guardsmen, thrusting and hacking, were torn from their steeds and beaten, stamped, and stabbed to death. Tananda, beset at last by terror, screamed as her horse reared. A score of wild black figures, men and women, clawed at her.

A giant grasped her thigh and plucked her from the saddle, full into the furious hands that eagerly awaited her. Her skirt was ripped from her body and waved in the air above her, while a bellow of primitive laughter went up from the surging mob. A woman spat in her face and tore off her breastplates, scratching her breasts with blackened fingernails. A hurtling stone grazed her head.

Tananda saw a stone clutched in a hand, whose owner sought to reach her in the press to brain her. Daggers glinted. Only the hindering numbers of the jammed mass kept them from instantly doing her to death. A roar went up: "To the temple of Jullah!"

An instant clamor responded. Tananda felt herself half carried, half dragged along by the surging mob. Black hands gripped her hair, arms, and legs. Blows aimed at her in the crush were blocked or diverted by the mass.

Then came a shock, under which the whole throng staggered, as a horseman on a powerful steed crashed full into the press. Men, screaming, went down to be crushed under the flailing hoofs. Tananda caught a glimpse of a figure towering above the throng, of a dark, scarred face under a steel helmet, and a great sword lashing up and down, spattering crimson splashes. But, from somewhere in the crowd, a spear licked upward, disemboweling the steed. It screamed, plunged, and went down.

The rider, however, landed on his feet, smiting right and left. Wildly driven spears glanced from his helmet or from the shield on his left arm, while his broadsword cleft flesh and bone, split skulls, and spilled entrails into the bloody dust.

Flesh and blood could not stand it. Clearing a space, the stranger stooped and caught up the terrified girl. Covering her with his shield, he fell back, cutting a ruthless path until he had backed into the angle of a wall. Pushing her behind him, he stood before her, beating back the frothing, screaming onslaught.

Then there was a clatter of hoofs. A company of guardsmen swept into the square, driving the rioters before them. The Kushites, screaming in sudden panic, fled into the side streets, leaving a score of bodies littering the square. The captain of the guard—a giant Negro, resplendent in crimson silk and gold-worked harness—approached and dismounted.

"You were long in coming," said Tananda, who had risen and regained her poise.

The captain turned ashy. Before he could move, Tananda had made a sign to the men behind him. Using both hands, one of them drove his spear between his captain's shoulders with such force that the point started out from his breast. The officer sank to his knees, and thrusts from a half-dozen more spears finished the task.

Tananda shook her long, black, disheveled hair and faced her rescuer. She was bleeding from a score of scratches and as naked as a newborn babe, but she stared at the man without perturbation or uncertainty. He gave back her stare, his expression betraying a frank admiration for her cool bearing and the ripeness of her brown limbs and voluptuously molded torso.

"Who are you?" she demanded.

"I am Conan, a Cimmerian," he grunted.

"Cimmerian?" She had never heard of his far country, which lay hundreds of leagues to the north. She frowned. "You wear Stygian mail and helm. Are you a Stygian of some sort?"

He shook his head, baring white teeth in a grin. "I got the armor from a Stygian, but I had to kill the fool first."

"What do you, then, in Meroê?"

"I am a wanderer," he said simply, "with a sword for hire. I came here to seek my fortune." He did not think it wise to tell her of his previous career as a corsair on the Black Coast, or of his chieftainship of one of the jungle tribes to the south.

The queen's eyes ran appraisingly over Conan's giant form, measuring the breadth of his shoulders and the depth of his chest. "I will hire your sword," she said at last. "What is your price?"

"What price do you offer?" he countered, with a rueful glance at the carcass of his horse. "I am a penniless wanderer and now, alas, afoot."

She shook her head. "No, by Set! You are penniless no longer, but captain of the royal guard. Will a hundred pieces of gold a month buy your loyalty?"

He glanced casually at the sprawling figure of the former captain, who lay in silk, steel, and blood. The sight did not dim the zest of his sudden grin.

"I think so," said Conan.

4. The Golden Slave

The days passed, and the moon waned and waxed. A brief, disorganized rising by the lower castes was put down by Conan with an iron hand. Shubba, Tuthmes' servant, returned to Meroê. Coming to Tuthmes in his chamber, where lion skins carpeted the marble floor, he said, "I have found the woman you desired, master—a Nemedian girl, captured from a trading vessel of Argos. I paid the Shemite slave trader many broad pieces of gold for her."

"Let me see her," commanded Tuthmes.

Shubba left the room and returned a moment later, leading a girl by the wrist. She was supple, and her white body formed a dazzling contrast to the brown and black bodies to which Tuthmes was accustomed. Her hair fell in a curly, rippling, golden stream over her white shoulders. She was clad only in a tattered shift. This Shubba removed, leaving her shrinking in complete nudity.

Impersonally, Tuthmes nodded. "She is a fine bit of merchandise. If I were not gambling for a throne, I might be tempted to keep her for myself. Have you taught her Kushite, as I commanded?"

"Aye; in the city of the Stygians and later, daily, on the caravan trail, I taught her. After the Shemite fashion, I impressed upon her the need of learning with a slipper. Her name is Diana."

Tuthmes seated himself on a couch and indicated that the girl should sit cross-legged on the floor at his feet. This she did.

"I am going to give you to the queen of Kush as a present," he said. "Nominally you will be her slave, but actually you will still belong to me. You will receive your orders regularly, and you shall not fail to carry them out. The queen is cruel and hasty, so beware of roiling her. You shall say nothing, even if tortured, of your continuing connection with me. Lest, when you fancy yourself out of my reach in the royal palace, you be tempted to disobey, I shall demonstrate my power to you."

Taking her hand, he led her through a corridor, down a flight of stone stairs, and into a long, dimly-lit room.

175

This chamber was divided into equal halves by a wall of crystal, as clear as water although a yard thick and strong enough to resist the lunge of a bull elephant. Tuthmes led Diana to this wall and made her stand, facing it, while he stepped back. Abruptly, the light went out.

As she stood in darkness, her slender limbs trembling with unreasoning panic, light began to glow out of the blackness. She saw a malformed, hideous head grow out of the blackness. She saw a bestial snout, chisel-like teeth, and bristles. As the horror moved toward her, she screamed and turned, forgetting in her frantic fear the sheet of crystal that kept the brute from her. In the darkness, she ran full into the arms of Tuthmes. She heard him hiss, "You have been my servant. Do not fail me, for if you do he will search you out wherever you may be. You cannot hide from him." When he whispered something else in her ear, she fainted.

Tuthmes carried her up the stairs and gave her into the hands of a black woman with orders to revive her, see that she had food and wine, and bathe, comb, perfume, and deck her for presentation to the queen on the morrow.

5. The Lash of Tananda

The next day, Shubba led Diana of Nemedia to Tuthmes' chariot, hoisted her into the car, and took the reins. It was a different Diana, scrubbed and perfumed, with her beauty enhanced by a discreet touch of cosmetics. She wore a robe of silk so thin that every contour could be seen through it. A diadem of silver sparkled on her golden hair.

She was, however, still terrified. Life had been a nightmare ever since the slavers had kidnapped her. She had tried to comfort herself, during the long months that followed, with the thought that nothing lasts forever and that things were so bad that they were bound to improve. Instead, they had only worsened.

Now she was about to be proffered as a gift to a cruel and irascible queen. If she survived, she would be caught between the dangers of Tuthmes' monster on one hand and the suspicions of the queen on the other. If she did not spy for Tuthmes, the demon would get her; if she did, the queen would probably catch her at it and have her done to death in some even more gruesome fashion.

Overhead, the sky had a steely look. In the west, clouds were piling up, tier upon tier; for the end of Kush's dry season was at hand.

The chariot rumbled toward the main square in front of the royal palace. The wheels crunched softly over drifted sand, now and then rattling loudly as they encountered a stretch of bare pavement. Few upper-caste Meroites were abroad, for the heat of the afternoon was at its height. Most of the ruling class slumbered in their houses. A few of their black servants slouched through the streets, turning blank faces, shining with sweat, toward the chariot as it passed.

At the palace, Shubba handed Diana down from the chariot and led her in through the gilded bronze gates. A fat major domo conducted them through corridors and into a large chamber, fitted out with the ornate opulence of the room of a Stygian princess—which in a way it was. On a couch of ivory and ebony, inlaid with gold and mother-of-pearl, sat Tananda, clad only in a brief skirt of crimson silk.

The queen's eyes insolently examined the trembling blond slave before her. The girl was obviously a fine piece of human property. But Tananda's heart, steeped in treachery itself, was swift to suspect treachery in others. The queen spoke suddenly, in a voice heavy with veiled menace:

"Speak, wench! Why did Tuthmes send you to the palace?"

"I—I do not know—where am I?—Who are you?" Diana had a small, high voice, like that of a child.

"I am Queen Tananda, fool! Now answer my question."

"I know not the answer, my lady. All I know is that Lord Tuthmes sent me as a gift—"

"You lie! Tuthmes is eaten up with ambition. Since he hates me, he would not make me a gift without an ulterior reason. He must have some plot in mind. Speak up, or it will be the worse for you!"

"I—I do not know! I do not know!" wailed Diana, bursting into tears. Frightened almost to insanity by Muru's demon, she could not have spoken even if she had wished. Her tongue would have refused to obey her brain.

"Strip her!" commanded Tananda. The flimsy robe was torn from Diana's body.

"String her up!" said Tananda. Diana's wrists were bound, the rope was thrown over a beam, and the end was pulled taut, so that the girl's arms were extended straight over her head.

Tananda rose, a whip in her hand. "Now," she said with a cruel smile, "we shall see what you know about our dear friend Tuthmes' little schemes. Once more: will you speak?"

Her voice choked with sobs, Diana could only shake her head. The whip wristled and cracked across the Nemedian girl's skin, leaving a red welt diagonally across her back. Diana uttered a piercing shriek.

"What's all this?" said a deep voice. Conan, wearing his coat of mail over his jubbah and girt with his sword, stood in the doorway. Having become intimate with Tananda, he was accustomed to entering her palace unannounced. Tananda had taken lovers before—the murdered Amboola among them—but never one in whose embraces she found such ecstasy, nor one whose relationship with her she flaunted so brazenly. She could not have enough of the giant northerner.

Now, however, she spun about. "Just a northern slut, whom Tuthmes was sending me as a gift—no doubt to slip a dagger into my ribs or a potion into my wine," she snapped. "I am trying to learn the truth from her. If you want to love me, come back later."

"That is not my only reason for coming," he replied, grinning wolfishly. "There is also a little matter of state. What is this folly, to let the blacks into the Inner City to watch Aahmes burn?"

"What folly, Conan? It will show the black dogs I am not to be trifled with. The scoundrel will be tortured in a way that will be remembered for years. Thus perish all foes of our divine dynasty! What objection have you, pray?"

"Just this: if you let a few thousand Kushites into the Inner City and then work up their blood lust by the sight of the torture, it won't take much to set off another rising. Your divine dynasty has not given them much cause to love it."

"I do not fear those black scum!"

"Maybe not. But I have saved your pretty neck from them twice, and the third time my luck might run out. I tried to tell your minister Afari this just now, in his palace, but he said it was your command and he could do naught. I thought you might listen to sense from me, since your people fear you too much to say anything that might displease you."

"I'll do naught of the kind. Now get out of here and leave me to my work—unless you would care to wield the whip yourself."

Conan approached Diana. "Tuthmes has taste," he

said. "But the lass has been frightened out of her wits. No tale you got out of her would be worth the hearing. Give her to me, and I'll show you what a little kindness can do."

"You, kind? Ha! Mind your own affairs, Conan, and I will mind mine. You should be posting your guardsmen against tonight's gathering." Tananda spoke sharply to Diana: "Now speak, hussy, damn your soul!" The whip hissed as she drew back her arm for another lash.

Moving with the effortless speed of a lion, Conan caught Tananda's wrist and twisted the whip out of her hand.

"Let me go!" she screamed. "You dare to use force on me? I'll have you—I'll—I'll—"

"You'll what?" said Conan calmly. He tossed the whip into a corner, drew his dagger, and cut the rope that bound Diana's wrists. Tananda's servants exchanged uneasy glances.

"Mind your royal dignity, Highness!" grinned Conan, gathering Diana into his arms. "Remember that, with me in command of the guard, you have at least a chance. Without me—well, you know the answer to that. I shall see you at the torture."

He strode toward the door, carrying the Nemedian girl. Screaming with rage, Tananda picked up the discarded whip and hurled it after him. The handle struck his broad back, and the whip fell to the floor.

"Just because she has a fish-belly skin like yours, you prefer her to me!" shrieked Tananda. "You shall rue your insolence!"

With a rumbling laugh, Conan walked out. Tananda sank to the floor, beating the marble with her fists and weeping with frustration.

Moments later, Shubba, driving Tuthmes' chariot back toward his master's house, passed Conan's dwelling. He was astonished to see Conan, carrying a naked girl in his arms, entering his front door. Shubba shook the reins and hastened on his way.

6. Dark Counsel

The first lamps had been lit against the dusk as Tuthmes sat in his chamber with Shubba and with Muru, the tall Kordafan sorcerer. Shubba, glancing uneasily at his master, had finished his tale.

"I see that I did not credit Tananda with her full measure of suspiciousness," said Tuthmes. "A pity to waste so promising an instrument as that Nemedian girl, but not every shaft strikes the butt. The question, however, is: what shall we do next? Has anyone seen Ageera?"

"Nay, my lord," said Shubba. "He vanished after stirring up that riot against Tananda—very prudently, if I may say so. Some say he has left Meroê; some, that he lurks in the temple of Jullah, working divinations by day and night."

"If our divine queen had the wit of a worm," sneered Tuthmes, "she would invade that devil-devil house with a few stout guardsmen and hang the priests to their own rooftree." His two companions started and shifted their eyes uneasily. "I know; you are all terrified of their spells and spooks. Well, let us see. The girl is now useless to us. If Tananda failed to wring our secrets from her, Conan will do so by gentler means, and in his house she will learn naught of interest to us anyway. She must die forthwith. Muru, can you send your demon to Conan's house while he is commanding his guardsmen this evening, to make away with the wench?"

"That I can, master," replied the Kordafan. "Should I not command it to stay there until Conan returns and slay him, too? For I see that you will never be king

181

whilst Conan lives. As long as he holds his present post, he will fight like a devil to protect the queen, his leman, because he so promised to do, regardless of how he and she may quarrel otherwise."

Shubba added: "Even if we got rid of Tananda, Conan would still stand in our way. He might become king himself. He is practically the uncrowned king of Kush now—the queen's confidant and lover. His guardsmen love him, swearing that despite his white skin he is really a black man like themselves inside."

"Good," said Tuthmes. "Let us dispose of the twain at the same time. I shall be watching the torture of Aahmes in the main square, so that none shall say that I had a hand in the slaying."

"Why not set the demon on Tananda, also?" asked Shubba.

"It is not yet time. First, I must align the other nobles behind my claim to the throne, and this will not be easy. Too many of them, as well, fancy themselves as king of Kush. Until my faction grows stronger, my hold on the throne would be as insecure as Tananda's now is. So I am satisfied to wait, meanwhile letting her hang herself by her own excesses."

7.   *The Fate of a Kingdom*

In the main square of the Inner City, Prince Aahmes was tied to a stake in the center. Aahmes was a plump, brown-skinned young man, whose very innocence in matters of politics, it seemed, had enabled Afari to trap him by a false accusation.

Bonfires in the corners of the square and lines of torches illuminated an infernal scene. Between the stake and the royal palace stood a low platform, on which sat Tananda. Around the platform, royal guards were ranked three deep.

The fires shone redly on the long blades of their spears, their shields of elephant hide, and the plumes of their headdresses.

To one side of the square, Conan sat his horse at the head of a company of mounted guardsmen with lances erect. In the distance, lightning rippled through high-piled clouds.

In the center, where Lord Aahmes was tied, more guardsmen kept a space clear. In the space, the royal executioner was heating the instruments of his calling over a little forge. The rest of the square was jammed with most of the folk of Meroê, mingled in one vast, indiscriminate throng. The torchlight picked out white eyeballs and teeth against dark skins. Tuthmes and his servants formed a solid clump in the front row.

Conan looked over the throng with dark foreboding All had been orderly so far; but who knew what would happen when primitive passions were stirred? A nameless anxiety nagged at the back of his mind. As time passed, this anxiety became fixed, not on the fate of the headstrong queen, but on the Nemedian girl whom he had left at his house. He had left her with only a single servant, a black woman, because he had needed all his guardsmen to control the gathering in the square.

In the few hours he had known Diana, Conan had become much taken with her. Sweet, gentle, and perhaps even a virgin, she contrasted in every way with the fiery, temptestuous, passionate, cruel, sensual Tananda. Being Tananda's lover was certainly exciting, but after a time Conan thought he might prefer someone less stormy for a change. Knowing Tananda, he would not have put it past her to have sent one of her servants to murder Diana while Conan was otherwise occupied.

In the center of the square, the executioner blew on his little charcoal fire with a bellows. He held up an instrument, which glowed a bright cherry red in the dark. He approached the prisoner. Conan could not hear over the murmur of the crowd, but he knew that the executioner was asking Aahmes for details of his plot. The captive shook his head.

It was as though a voice were speaking inside Conan's mind, urging him to return to his house. In the Hyborian lands, Conan had listened to the speculations of priests and philosophers. They had argued over the existence of guardian spirits and over the possibility of direct communication from mind to mind. Being convinced that they were all mad, he had not paid much attention at the time. Now, however, he thought he knew what they were talking about. He tried to dismiss the sensation as mere imagination; but it returned, stronger than ever.

At last Conan told his adjutant: "Mongo, take command until I return."

"Whither go you, Lord Conan?" asked the black.

"To ride through the streets, to be sure no gang of rascals has gathered under cover of darkness. Keep things under control; I shall soon be back."

Conan turned his horse and trotted out of the square. The crowd opened to let him pass. The sensation in his head was stronger than ever. He clucked his steed to an easy canter and presently drew rein in front of his dwelling. A faint rumble of thunder sounded.

The house was dark, save for a single light in the back. Conan dismounted, tied his horse, and entered, hand on hilt. At that instant he heard a frightful scream, which he recognized as the voice of Diana.

With a sulfurous oath, Conan rushed headlong into the house, tearing out his sword. The scream came from the living room, which was dark save for the stray beams of a single candle that burned in the kitchen.

At the door of the living room, Conan halted, transfixed by the scene before him. Diana cowered on a low settee strewn with leopard skins, her white limbs unveiled by the disarray of her silken shift. Her blue eyes were dilated with terror.

Hanging in the center of the room, a gray, coiling mist was taking shape and form. The seething fog had already partly condensed into a hulking, monstrous form with sloping, hairy shoulders and thick, bestial limbs. Conan glimpsed the creature's misshapen head with its bristling, piglike snout and tusked, champing jaws.

The thing had solidified out of thin air, materializing by some demonic magic. Primal legends rose in Conan's mind—whispered tales of horrid, shambling things that prowled the dark and slew with inhuman fury. For half a heartbeat his atavistic fears made him hesitate. Then, with a snarl of rage, he sprang forward to give battle—and tripped over the body of the black woman servant, who had fainted and lay just inside the doorway. Conan fell sprawling, the sword flying from his hand.

At the same instant the monster, with supernatural quickness, whirled and launched itself at Conan in a gigantic bound. As Conan fell flat, the demon passed clear over his body and fetched up against the wall of the hall outside.

The combatants were on their feet in an instant. As the monster sprang upon Conan anew, a flash of lightning outside gleamed upon its great chisel tusks. The Cimmerian thrust his left elbow up under its jaw, while he fumbled with his right hand for his dagger.

The demon's hairy arms encircled Conan's body with crushing force; a smaller man's back would have been broken. Conan heard his clothing rip as the blunt nails of its hands dug in, and a couple of links of his mail shirt snapped with sharp, metallic sounds. Although the weight of the demon was about the same as the Cim-

185

merian's, its strength was incredible. As he strained every muscle, Conan felt his left forearm being bent slowly back, so that the snouted jaws came closer and closer to his face.

In the semidark, the two stamped and staggered about like partners in some grotesque dance. Conan fumbled for his dagger, while the demon brought its tusks ever nearer. Conan realized that his belt must have become awry, so that the dagger was out of reach. He felt even his titanic strength ebbing, when something cold was thrust into his groping right hand. It was the hilt of his sword, which Diana had picked up and now pressed into his grasp.

Drawing back his right arm, Conan felt with his point for a place in the body of his assailant. Then he thrust. The monster's skin seemed of unnatural toughness, but a mighty heave drove the blade home. Spasmodically champing its jaws, the creature uttered a bestial grunt.

Conan stabbed again and again, but the shaggy brute did not even seem to feel the bite of the steel. The demonic arms dragged the Cimmerian into an ever closer, bone-crushing embrace. The chisel-toothed jaws came closer and closer to his face. More links of his mail shirt parted with musical snapping sounds. Rough claws ripped his tunic and dug bloody furrows in his sweat-smeared back. A viscous fluid from the creature's wounds, which did not feel like any normal blood, ran down the front of Conan's garments.

At length, doubling both legs and driving them into the thing's belly with every ounce of strength remaining to him, Conan tore himself free. He staggered to his feet, dripping gore. As the demon shuffled toward him again, swinging its apelike arms for another grapple, Conan, with both hands on his hilt, swung his sword in a desperate arc. The blade bit into the monster's neck, half severing it. The mighty blow would have decapitated two or even three human foes at once, but the demon's tissues were tougher than those of mortal men.

The demon staggered back and crashed to the floor. As Conan stood panting, with dripping blade, Diana threw her arms about his neck. "I'm so glad—I prayed to Ishtar to send you—"

"There, there," said Conan, comforting the girl with rough caresses. "I may look ready for the grave, but I can still stand—"

He broke off, eyes wide. The dead thing rose, its malformed head wobbling on its half-severed neck. It lurched to the door, tripped over the still-unconscious body of the Negro servant woman, and staggered out into the night.

"Crom and Mitra!" gasped Conan. Pushing the girl aside, he growled: "Later, later! You're a good lass, but I must follow that thing. That's the demon of the night they talk about, and by Crom, I'll find out where it comes from!"

He reeled out, to find his horse gone. A length of rein attached to the hitching ring told that the animal had broken its tether in panic at the demon's appearance.

Moments later. Conan reappeared in the square. As he rammed his way through the crowd, which had burst into a roar of excitement, he saw the monster stagger and fall in front of the tall Kordafan wizard in Tuthmes' group. In its final throes, it laid its head at the sorcerer's feet.

Screams of rage arose from the crowd, which recognized the monster as the demon that for years had terrified Meroê from time to time. Although the guardsmen still struggled to keep the space around the torture stake open, hands reached from the sides and back to pull Muru down. In the confused uproar, Conan caught a few snatches of speech: "Slay him! He is the demon's master! Kill him!"

A sudden hush fell. In the clear space, Ageera had suddenly appeared, his shaven head painted to resemble a skull. It was as if he had somehow bounded over the heads of the crowd to land in the clearing.

"Why slay the tool and not the man who wields it?" he shrieked. He pointed at Tuthmes. "There stands he whom the Kordafan served! At his command, the demon slew Amboola! My spirits have told me, in the silence of the temple of Jullah! Slay him, too!"

As more hands dragged down the screaming Tuthmes, Ageera pointed toward the platform on which sat the queen. "Slay all the lords! Cast off your bonds! Kill the masters! Be free men again and not slaves! Kill, kill, kill!"

Conan could barely keep his feet in the buffeting of the crowd, which surged this way and that, chanting: "Kill, kill, kill!" Here and there a screaming lord was brought down and torn to pieces.

Conan struggled toward his mounted guards, by means of whom he still hoped to clear the square. Then, over the heads of the mob, he saw a sight that changed his plans. A royal guardsman, standing with his back to the platform, turned about and hurled his spear straight at the queen, whom he was supposed to protect. The spear went through her glorious body as if through butter. As she slumped in her seat, a dozen more spears found their mark in her. At the fall of their ruler, the mounted guardsmen joined the rest of the tribesmen in the massacre of the ruling caste.

Moments later, Conan, battered and disheveled but leading another horse, appeared at his dwelling. He tied the animal, rushed inside, and brought a bag of coins out of its hiding place.

"Let's go!" he barked at Diana. "Grab a loaf of bread!

Where in the cold Hells of Niflheim is my shield? Ah, here!"

"But don't you want to take those nice things—"

"No time; the browns are done for. Hold my girdle while you ride behind me. Up with you, now!"

With its double burden, the horse galloped heavily through the Inner City, through a rabble of looters and rioters, pursuers and pursued. One man, who leaped for the animal's bridle, was ridden down with a shriek and a snapping of bones; others scrambled madly out of the way. Out through the great bronze gates they rode, while behind them the houses of the nobility blazed up into yellow pyramids of flame. Overhead lightning flashed, thunder roared, and rain came pelting down like a waterfall.

An hour later, the rain had slackened to a drizzle. The horse moved at a slow walk, picking its way through the darkness.

"We're still on the Stygian road," grumbled Conan, striving to pierce the dark with his gaze. "When the rain stops, we'll stop, too, to dry off and get a little sleep."

"Where are we going?" said the high, gentle voice of Diana.

"I don't know; but I'm tired of the black countries. You cannot do anything with these people; they are as hide-bound and as thick-headed as the barbarians of my own north country—the Cimmerians and Æsir and Vanir. I am minded to have another try at civilization."

"And what about me?"

"What do you want? I'll send you home or keep you with me, whichever you like."

"I think," she said in a small voice, "that in spite of the wet and everything, I like things as they are."

Conan grinned silently in the darkness and urged the horse to a trot.

The Immortal Warrior.
The Legend.
Conan

__CONAN #1	0-441-11481-4/$4.50
__CONAN OF CIMMERIA #2	0-441-11453-9/$4.50
__CONAN THE FREEBOOTER #3	0-441-11863-1/$3.50
__CONAN THE ADVENTURER #5	0-441-11858-5/$3.50
__CONAN THE BUCCANEER #6	0-441-11585-3/$3.50
__CONAN THE USURPER #8	0-441-11589-6/$3.50
__CONAN THE AVENGER #10	0-441-11483-0/$3.95
__CONAN OF AQUILONIA #11	0-441-11484-9/$3.95
__CONAN OF THE ISLES #12	0-441-11623-X/$3.95
__CONAN THE SWORDSMAN #13	0-441-11479-2/$3.95
__CONAN THE LIBERATOR #14	0-441-11617-5/$3.95
__CONAN #15: THE SWORD OF SKELOS	0-441-11480-6/$3.95
__CONAN #16: THE ROAD OF KINGS	0-441-11618-3/$3.95
__CONAN THE REBEL #17	0-441-11642-6/$3.95